LISTENING FOR JUPITER

Pierre-Luc Landry

LISTENING
FOR JUPITER

Translated from the French by
Arielle Aaronson (Xavier's sections)
and Madeleine Stratford (Hollywood's sections)

QC FICTION

Revision: Peter McCambridge
Proofreading: Elizabeth West, David Warriner
Book design and ebooks: Folio infographie
Cover & logo: Maison 1608 by Solisco
Fiction editor: Peter McCambridge

Copyright © 2016 Éditions Druide inc.
Originally published under the title *Les corps extraterrestres*

Translation Copyright © Arielle Aaronson, Madeleine Stratford

ISBN 978-177186-098-7 pbk; 978-1-77186-099-4 epub; 978-1-77186-100-7 pdf; 978-1-77186-101-4 mobi/pocket

Legal Deposit, 2nd quarter 2016

Bibliothèque et Archives nationales du Québec
Library and Archives Canada

Published by QC Fiction
6977, rue Lacroix
Montréal, Québec H4E 2V4
Telephone: 514 808-8504
QC@QCfiction.com
www.QCfiction.com

QC Fiction is an imprint of Baraka Books.

Printed and bound in Québec

Trade Distribution & Returns
Canada and the United States
Independent Publishers Group
1-800-888-4741 (IPG1);
orders@ipgbook.com

Société
de développement
des entreprises
culturelles
Québec

We acknowledge the support from the Société de développement des entreprises culturelles (SODEC) and the Government of Quebec tax credit for book publishing administered by SODEC.

Financé par le gouvernement du Canada
Funded by the Government of Canada | Canada

We acknowledge the financial support of the Government of Canada through the National Translation Program for Book Publishing, an initiative of the Roadmap for Canada's Official Languages 2013-2018: Education, Immigration, Communities, for our translation activities.

"One by one the stars fell into the sea, the sky drained of its last lights."

Albert Camus (tr. Ryan Bloom)
Notebooks, 1951-59

"Fiction imitates fiction."

Marc Augé (tr. Liz Heron)
The War of Dreams

"I cannot sleep. I dream that I am in a bed, elsewhere, and that I cannot sleep. I wake. I now know I was asleep. But I am not anymore, and now I really cannot sleep."

Roger Caillois
The Uncertainty That Comes From Dreams

Part one

Xavier

WE'RE ALL GOING TO DIE. That's what crossed my mind while the car was idling. I thought: all these people—Earth's entire population, me, them, everybody—we're all going to die at some point. The end is the cornerstone of our very existence. It's cliché, of course, but it caught me off guard and kind of knocked the wind out of me. I closed my eyes and counted to ten. I thought: if I open my eyes and everything is still there, if nothing's changed, it means I won't die today. I opened them.

"Oh, get out of the way, you twit! Bloody hell! Can't you just stay home if you're afraid of a little snow, arsehole?"

The taxi driver was getting impatient. But the traffic didn't bother me. Neither did the cold.

OK, I should be honest: the snowstorm worried me a bit. A tiny little bit. I'd started to believe that maybe it was as bad as the media claimed when the plane had to circle Heathrow for more than two hours before the pilot got permission to land. But I wasn't going to complain about the delay; I didn't feel like preparing the London pitch, or the one for the Bilbao convention the following week. I wanted to let these "extraordinary circumstances," these "historic snowfalls" pin me down. I would hide myself amid the crowd and make London my own haven of idleness. But worry had nevertheless crept up on me.

Antony had left me a message a few hours earlier. He wouldn't meet me at the hotel until the next day, because he'd had to sleep in Lisbon; no planes had been allowed to take off and the airport had just closed. He would take the train to Paris, if all went well, and then a coach on to London.

The company had rented us two rooms at the Hilton across from Hyde Park with a partial view of the garden. The Royal College of Physicians conference would be held there. I had to meet with a group of cardiologists on Tuesday to present a new calcium blocker for patients with Raynaud's syndrome, a product that was less harmful to the liver than current drugs, to be prescribed to elderly patients suffering from hepatic failure. The thought was weighing on me, and I just wanted to sink into a chair facing the window and watch the snow fall onto the trees lining the pond while drinking a scalding cup of tea. I was already fed up with calcium blockers, even though I'd only been presenting the product for a few months. Before that, it was a new type of non-drowsy antianxiety medication. Before that, amoxicillin for viral lung diseases in children.

The taxi driver honked. We were at a complete stand-still. The car in front of us had been abandoned, its doors wide open.

"How long before we reach the hotel?" I asked.

"Usually less than two minutes by cab. But the twit here left his car in the middle of the road."

I handed him a £50 note and got out of the car, asking him to bring my bags to the hotel as soon as possible. I closed the door behind me. I wanted to walk the rest of the way. I'd get to the hotel sooner and I'd be able to enjoy that partial view of the garden.

At least twenty centimetres of snow covered the pavement. I wasn't wearing boots; cold water soaked through my shoes, pants and wool coat. I couldn't see where I was going through the strong wind. On the right, I passed the entrance to Notting Hill Gate Tube station, then the intersection of Kensington Church Street.

We're all going to die, I kept thinking. All this snow must be some sort of sign.

My phone rang.

"Xavier?"

It was Antony. There was static on the line, probably because of the storm.

"Yes."

"I ended up taking a train to Paris. I'll get to London tomorrow, in time for the pitch. *Et toi*?"

"I'm OK. I'll be at the hotel in a few minutes. I'll let them know you've been held up."

"*Pas besoin*, I already called them. See you tomorrow, then."

He hung up right away. My forehead was numb from the wind and my clothes were soaked and frozen.

"Sir, please. Do you know if the Hilton hotel is in this neighbourhood?"

The man I'd just stopped raised his head to look at me.

"It's just around the corner, mate."

He pointed to the next intersection, barely visible through the blizzard. A two-minute walk, at most. I didn't notice, but Notting Hill Gate had become Bayswater Road. I started to run, stumbling at every step.

Snow clung to the hotel's brick façade, which had turned white like everything else: buildings, trees, road signs. A doorman let me in and I collapsed against the reception desk, out of breath.

"Hi. I have a room here. My name is Xavier Adam."

: :

I turned on the TV after stripping off my wet clothes. I hadn't seen *Annie Hall* in forever, even though I always say it's my favourite movie. I called room service and asked them to bring me tea and gummy bears. I don't know who I think I am; I like to act like they do in the movies. Plus, the company's paying.

I didn't take my eyes off the movie until it was over; I read all of the closing credits, or almost. Then I turned off the TV. It was late, I hadn't eaten—other than the

14

gummy bears—and I didn't feel like going out. I called room service again and asked them to bring me a meal. I slipped into the robe patterned with the hotel colours, opened the window to let in some air and lay down on the rug, between the bed and the TV. There was a knock at the door.

The attendant came in with a tray on a small cart, just like in the movies. I motioned to the nightstand. "Thanks."

She left soundlessly and I didn't get up until the door was completely shut. I wanted to seem as disagreeable, as irritating as possible. I thought: I'll take a midnight dip, then I'll ask them to bring a bottle of scotch up to my room. Even though I don't really like scotch. I'll be like Bill Murray in *Lost in Translation*.

I lifted the cover off the dish. They'd brought me a stew, brown mush that smelled of boiled beef, along with a bread roll. I ate on the bed, shivering. Then I got up, closed the window and ran a scalding-hot bath. But I changed my mind right away and drained the tub before so much as dipping a toe in.

I went swimming. And afterwards I asked for a bottle of scotch to be brought to my room.

The storm didn't let up during the night. It got even worse. Fuck the snow, I thought. I threw on some jeans over my pyjamas, along with two T-shirts, a wool sweater and my coat, and went down to the lobby. I bought a giant fur hat, a huge scarf and two pairs of gloves at a store a few steps from the hotel. I felt like walking, visiting Hyde Park, taking some time for myself outside of work. It was pretty good timing; Antony hadn't arrived yet and I'd left my phone in the room.

I walked up and down the paths until I was breathless with hunger. Then I let myself fall backwards into the snow and decided to freeze to death. I knew I'd only have to take a few steps in the right direction to get back to the hotel, but I was in the mood for a little tragedy. Unfortunately, a passerby saw me collapse and came straight over to help. Let me die in peace, I wanted to tell him, but my chin was completely frozen, along with my lower lip. My throat was dry, despite all the snow I'd swallowed, and I was too short of breath to say a word. I pointed to the hotel in the distance, behind the veil of white powder, and the man put his arm around my shoulders to help me walk over.

"Bless your soul," I told him when he left me in the lobby.

I was feeling mystical. Spiritual, at the very least. The man grumbled something like "Be careful next time" and left. An employee came running over to ask if I wanted him to call an ambulance. No need. Anyway, with the storm, I would have been surprised to see the emergency medics rushing to the Hilton for a snowman who'd tried to let himself freeze to death in a park. "I'll take a hot bath." He helped me to the elevator and asked if he could bring something up to my room, on the house. No thanks, I don't need anything. But wait. Why not? A bottle of champagne, maybe?

In the bath, I belted out the biggest hits in my repertoire: Gainsbourg's *Comic Strip*, Madonna's *Hollywood* and Velvet Underground's *Pale Blue Eyes*. And I didn't think about a thing. It felt incredibly good.

My phone rang. I didn't pick up; I was in no shape to stand and walk over to where I'd put it down earlier. Then, after a minute, someone knocked on the door.

"It's open!" I yelled.

"Xavier?"

"Here!" I shouted, still motionless. "Did you just leave me a message?"

"Yeah," Antony replied, walking into the room. "I just got in."

I dragged myself out of the bath with considerable effort and leaned against the counter so I wouldn't fall. My legs were still wobbly, paralyzed from the cold.

"Fuck, Xavier! You're naked, man!"

Antony threw me the robe that was lying on the bed and turned to face the window.

"I know. I was in the bath."

I took a step and collapsed on the floor.

"Can you help me get to the bed?"

"What's wrong with you?"

"My legs are all frozen and numb."

"How come?"

"I was outside. I went for a walk."

Antony helped me get up and I was able to sit on the bed.

"You went for a walk—*avec cette neige?*"

"Yeah."

"You're crazy! Anyway... Pullman called and told me tomorrow's meeting is still on. *T'es prêt?*"

The idea wasn't appealing. I'd secretly been hoping the meeting would be called off and we'd get to enjoy London in the snow, that all international flights would be cancelled and we'd have to stay here indefinitely. That time would stop for good, that the Hilton staff would take care of me, that I'd be able to watch movies all night and sleep all day and swim whenever I wanted and walk around naked in the room without closing the curtains or anything.

"Yeah. I think so."

"What do you mean you think so? *T'es prêt ou pas?*"

"I think so."

Antony was going to lose it, I could tell.

"Xavier, shit. This meeting is really important. If they buy the drug we get a promotion, which means I get to pay my mortgage and make my wife happy and have great sex when I get home. I need to be made junior associate, and you don't want to stand in my way."

"I know, you already told me all this."

He was getting ready to leave.

"I don't know what's with you lately, but you better be ready tomorrow. I can call a whore for you, if that's what you need to get a little excited about life and stuff."

I motioned for him to let it go, and he left.

I turned on the TV and picked a channel at random. *Reality Bites* had been on for about an hour. I got the feeling that it was no coincidence, turning on the TV like that, right at that moment, choosing that channel—among so many others—happening on this part of the movie in particular, on this dialogue between Lelaina Pierce and Troy Dyer:

Lelaina Pierce: "I was really going to be somebody by the time I was twenty-three."

Troy Dyer: "Honey, all you have to be by the time you're twenty-three is yourself."

Lelaina Pierce: "I don't know who that is anymore."

It hit me and hit me hard; if I hadn't been lying in bed, I'd have probably fallen over. I'm just like Lelaina: I don't have any idea who I am, and I still haven't become someone great, someone good.

I've been going around in circles. I think about what I'd like to do rather than sell medication. I'm tired of feeling sorry for myself. I've had enough of these hotel rooms and convention centres. I want my life to have meaning, but I don't know where to find it—or where to look. I can rattle off expressions like "vaso-constrictor tone," "myocardial oxygen consumption" and "supraventricular tachycardia," when in reality I have no idea what I'm talking about and couldn't care less. I want to scream, tell the whole world how much it pisses me off, give it a black eye. I've put some money aside, I could make it a few months without working, a year maybe. The idea is becoming an obsession.

I watched the movie through to the end. Then I turned off the screen and collapsed from exhaustion. It was almost five in the morning.

Xavier

I want my story to be beautiful—not realistic—by the time I'm ready to share it. For it to be extraordinary, even with its inconsistencies and holes. Yet I have nothing incredible to tell. The extraordinary, that's the stuff we never question. The real, the things we claim to know and can explain. I'm looking for my own connection to one of these possible truths, one to be mine, to help me understand the world. Here in this notebook I have to put into words the sort of incongruity I feel when confronted with real things. Try to dig through the nagging feeling that what passes for normal is, in fact, not. I think I should go back to school, like Annie Hall. Lelaina and Alvy read the classics; not me. So, twenty-four entries already and I can barely even put the signs of my unease into words.

I had the same dream again. I say 'the same,' but that isn't true. It never happens in exactly the same way. And the conversations are always different. I have this recurring dream so often it makes me wonder: Who is this guy I only see at night? The next time he appears, I'll ask him. Yes: tonight, I'll ask his name.

Hollywood

I WASN'T HOME WHEN SHE GOT THERE. I was at the park, despite the warning signs at the gate: "Access prohibited after 11 p.m. Minimum fine: $100." It was hot out, more than twenty-five degrees, even though it was night, and winter—March soon and it hadn't even snowed yet. Summer didn't want to end and I, for one, liked it that way because I could spend the night outside without worrying about freezing to death. I was lying on a wooden bridge in a playground, listening to *Everybody Knows* on my iPod and looking for the stars. They're harder to find in the city. The sky is brown or purple or orange or pink and you can only see the moon, and Venus when there are no clouds. Sometimes, later at night, you can catch a glimpse of Jupiter. One day, I'd like to go up north, to the top of a mountain or to an island. I'd lie down in the tall grass and stay up all night, gazing at the sky to see at last what Alpha Centauri, Sirius and Canis Major actually look like.

When I got home a little after midnight, she was sitting at the kitchen table with my mom. They were both drinking coffee, even though it was late.

My mom was wiping tears off her cheeks and Saké seemed to be comforting her.

"What's up?" I asked.

I couldn't hear my mom's answer. I took out my earbuds, asking her to say it again.

"My parents are missing," said Saké, smiling at me.

"You remember Saké?" my mom asked.

I remembered her well. We'd grown up together; our mothers had been childhood friends. I hadn't seen her for years, though. These things happen.

"Sure! But... uh... what?"

I cleared my throat and started over. "I mean: they're *missing*? What happened?"

My mom burst into tears and hiccupped an answer. "Nobody knows. They've been gone for two weeks. They went off to work one morning and never came back."

At which point my dad came in.

"Oh! Hollywood, there you are. I've been looking everywhere for you," he said, tossing his car keys on the buffet before sitting down next to mom at the kitchen table. Saké got up and came to greet me with a kiss.

"It's been a while! How've you been?"

"Um... Well, I guess. You?"

24

"I'm OK. I'll pretend to be sad for a few days," she said conspiratorially, "'cause the truth is, I don't really care. I mean: as long as my folks are alive... I wouldn't like to learn that they're dead or in pain, or they've been kidnapped or whatever, but if they took off like that 'cause they just felt like it, well, good for them. I'm old enough to take care of myself. I came here 'cause the house feels too big for me, all by myself. So I thought I'd crash at your parents', and they said yes. Other than that, it's all good."

Saké had changed a lot, but I wasn't surprised to see what she'd become. She was wearing a pair of tight black jeans with lots of holes in them and a sweatshirt that was way too big for her, like Jennifer Beals' on the *Flashdance* poster, hanging over her shoulder and puffy at the waist. Her hair was dyed black and purple, teased into a bun and styled with a kind of paste or gel, or something.

At that moment, I felt a sharp pain. I had to sit down. Some kind of cramp in my ribcage. Nothing to do with Saké's sudden return; it just happens to me sometimes, ever since the surgery. When I wake up, mostly, but also when I'm tired or stressed out, or annoyed with something. Or else for no reason at all. Like now, standing in the dining room, after midnight, looking at Saké as she tells me how little she cares about her parents vanishing mysteriously. It's as if my bones were trying to break out of my body in search of the heart that the doctors took out. To "cure that weariness and gloom we've been unable to treat," they said. Well, I haven't noticed any change in my attitude since. Besides, I've never complained before; I am quite content with my own state of mind. It was my parents who insisted I meet with a social worker when I was in high school, and then with a psychologist in college. And then with a psychiatrist the psychologist referred me to. And then with a second psychiatrist, who realized my heart had stopped beating and sent me to a heart surgeon who wanted to see his name in large print in a journal of experimental medicine. He must be quite pleased with himself: I am the only human being on Earth to live without a heart. He and his colleagues took out a useless organ: my blood flows all the same, and that's just the way it is. I haven't mentioned the cramps to my parents because I know they'd insist I make an appointment with the surgeon, and I don't feel like seeing him again, not before my yearly checkup. When I get one, I find a place to sit and breathe slowly. The pain usually subsides after a few minutes. But if I have to pretend that I'm all right so as not to scare my parents or make a scene, for instance, the cramp can last a little longer, and sometimes the pain is so unbearable that I have to run and hide, coming up with some excuse to leave the room. Since Saké wouldn't stop talking, telling me how she got kicked out of college, how she'd become a model for a shampoo company, how she'd managed to leave her ex—a small-time crook who'd steal washers and dryers from department stores, paying with fake credit cards—how she'd been admitted to another college; anyway, since she just wouldn't stop talking, I couldn't concentrate on the pain and make it go away. I had to get out of the kitchen and lock myself in the bathroom, claiming I'd downed three bottles of water and really had to take a leak.

The pain finally subsided but I stayed locked in the bathroom a good ten minutes longer, listening to *Dance Me to the End of Love* in the bathtub. At times like these, I want only one thing: to lie on my back and listen to Leonard Cohen. Which reminds me: in grade 10, a mental health professional came to our Personal and Social Development class to talk about the shelter where she worked. Her beneficiaries, as she called them, would listen to the same song or watch the same movie three or four times in a row, without growing tired of it. I don't know if she meant this was a sign of mental illness, but it hit home. So I listened to *Dance Me to the End of Love* two or three times over before coming out of the bathroom. Saké was waiting for me at the door.

"What were you doing in there?"

"Listening to music."

"Ah."

My mom shouted from the kitchen: "Hollywood, would you show Saké to the guest room?"

"Yes, Mom."

Saké laughed.

"You still call her 'Mom'?"

"What else should I call her?"

"Her name!"

I shrugged and walked to the guest room at the end of the hallway.

"There. This is it."

"Thanks."

I let Saké into her bedroom and made for my own. But she turned back right away and took me by the arm.

"Wait. You're going to bed already?"

"No, I'm not tired."

"Me neither."

"Want to eat something?"

"Sure! Why not?"

We went back to the kitchen. My parents were still at the table. Mom had stopped crying, but she was still sniffling.

"Are you kids hungry?" she asked, as if she were reading our minds.

"Yes."

"You should order takeout."

I looked at Saké.

"Chinese?" she suggested.

Mom got up and opened the drawer where we keep all the restaurant menus.

"You could order from Kim Moon Kim's, it's open all night," she said, handing Saké the menu.

My mom called the restaurant and placed our orders before going to bed. Saké chose beef chow mein, my dad, shrimp chop suey, and I went for vegetable fried rice. We waited playing cards, then we ate our food listening to a stupid show on the radio. I'd wanted to put on a record, *I'm Your Man*, but Dad had insisted on listening to what those people had to say. As I expressed my doubts about hotlines, my dad, for form's sake, told me to shut up and eat. Saké seemed to think we were behaving like idiots. Still, I thought it was weird that her parents' disappearance should leave her so cold. I didn't want to ask her about it and I was hoping my dad would; instead, he asked what she'd been up to. She talked about her work as a hair show model and about her studies in cinema, sculpture and graphic design, and then she stopped and stared at me for a while without saying a word.

"Hollywood! You have to come to the studio with me on Monday!" she blurted out. "I'm sure they'll want to sign you on. We never have enough guys in our shows, plus you have crazy hair. They'll want you for sure!"

I pouted as I tossed my Styrofoam tray into the trash, and I left the kitchen to go lock myself in my room. I took off my clothes and lay down over the covers because I was hot. I pressed my iPod earbuds in and listened to two whole Leonard Cohen albums, *New Skin for the Old Ceremony* and *Songs of Love and Hate*, but I couldn't fall asleep. I put my clothes back on and quietly left the apartment.

Outside, I walked over to the grocery store and stepped into the phone booth near the entrance. I dialed Chokichi's number. He lives close by, so he came to meet me right in the parking lot.

"There you go," he said, handing me a small bag. "Ten Gardenal tablets. Just take one. It works better up the rectum, but I suppose you'd rather swallow."

29

I paid; he pocketed the cash. He stayed and we talked for a while, sitting on the narrow strip of sidewalk between the parking lot and a flowerbed that had seen better days. I told him about Saké. He mentioned a mutual friend he'd had a fling with a few days earlier, after trying out a shipment of contraband Viagra. Chokichi is into trafficking. He's a petty independent drug dealer and a trusted friend. My only friend, in fact, for lack of a better term.

Chokichi left around 4 a.m. I went home, took a Gardenal and fell asleep about twenty minutes later.

I woke up at 1:30 p.m. My parents had gone to work hours earlier. Saké was nowhere to be seen. She'd left a note for me inside the fridge:

Hollywood,

I'm off to school. I have multimedia production until noon and sculpture in the afternoon. Your mom said you'd be working until 10 at the graveyard. Seriously? What are you? A tomb raider?

Anyway, in case you're interested, I'm going to a friend's house tonight to watch an Asian horror flick her boyfriend brought back from Thailand. I'll come and pick you up around 10:30.

See you tonight!
Saké

I folded the note and put it in my pocket. I poured myself a glass of chocolate milk and took a straw from the utensil drawer. I sat down in front of the TV to watch a documentary on Jupiter's Great Red Spot, a massive anticyclone that was first seen almost two hundred years ago and still looks the same today. The scientists who were interviewed compared it to a never-ending hurricane with winds raging at over 550 kilometres per hour. The more they study the phenomenon, they said, the less they understand it.

::

I finished work earlier that night because no burial service was scheduled in my section on the weekend, which meant no lot to weed, no digging to authorize, nothing complicated to do. I raked the aisles, picked up some rocks and, once I was sure that nobody could see me, took a few seeds out of my jacket pocket and planted them in front of two or three gravestones. Green beans. It came to me a short while ago. Since summer is everlasting, or has been for the past ten months anyway—twenty-five degrees Celsius last February and no ground frost in over a year—in short, because Montreal is turning into Los Angeles, it's easy to grow beans anytime, and the wheat is always golden. I bought a big bag of *Phaseolus vulgaris*, a common bean, at the market. I try and plant seeds in front of at least two gravestones after every shift. At this rate, in a few months, when the seeds have sprouted and the plants have grown, my whole section will be like one big bean garden. Unless winter comes back, bringing an end to the soon-to-be year-long summer.

I walked home instead of taking the metro or the bus because it was nice and hot out and I was in no hurry. I went into a café that was still open and bought an avocado and alfalfa sandwich that I ate while I walked. I stopped in front of our building to pull up some dried-up shoots. Ours is the only building on the street not to stand directly beside the others. The landlord, who had it built about forty years earlier, had always wanted to live on a farm and grow grains. So he had it stand off the street, a few metres away from the neighbours, and he planted wheat all around. It's really ugly, all the more so because he's too old to look after the crop, but won't get rid of it. I look after the "garden" in exchange for a bit off the monthly rent. My parents made the deal with the landlord a few years ago to teach me "the feeling of satisfaction that comes with a job well done." I was a teenager then, and they thought I was going off the rails because I never talked to them. I pull up dead plants and sow a few seeds when the garden looks like it needs it. I'm not sure what type of grain it is. I've never taken the trouble, after all these years, to look into what we could do with all those plants. I just gather the stems, without pulling out the ears, and leave them in front of the landlord's apartment door. The wheat vanishes every time, without me seeing whether he's picked it up and brought it in himself or whether the janitor gets rid of it when he sweeps our hallway. What I like most about the work is how it lets me see the sparrows up close as they eat the grain. I can watch them for hours as they pick at the wheat, hopping and chirping around.

Saké was waiting for me upstairs, in our fifth-floor apartment. She was in my dad's armchair in the living room, drinking orange juice and watching the evening news.

"My parents aren't back yet?" I asked.

"Yeah, but they've gone out. To the movies."

"Ah. Well... Still on for tonight?"

"Absolutely! Rajani emailed me the trailer for the movie. A bit dumb, but oh so gory!"

She got up and I followed her into the study. She ran the trailer for me.

"A *bit* dumb? Your run-of-the-mill low-budget horror flick, but in Thai."

"Just you wait and see. They're about to take part in this satanic ritual. They'll stick hooks into their skin all over their bodies, even into their eyeballs."

I waited. In the end, she was right: the movie was pretty gory, really disgusting. I wasn't too keen on watching it, but out of curiosity, I asked her what time her friend was expecting us.

"We can leave now, if you're ready."

"I'm ready. Where does she live?"

"Not too far."

We walked to Rajani's. She rented the basement of a small townhouse with her boyfriend, a computer, IC, or electronics engineer, or all three at once; an engineer, at any rate. Rajani studied Medieval Latin and History at university, up on the hill. She and Saké had met in college, before Saké was expelled. We talked a little before putting on the movie. Actually, Saké was the one who talked. Rajani asked questions, and I listened. Arnaud, Rajani's boyfriend, was making goat cheese pizza for us to eat during the movie. I tried to swallow a couple of bites like everybody else, but was put off by the graphic scenes. Saké ate at least three slices. After the movie, Arnaud told us about his trip to Thailand. He'd been sent by the company he worked for to set up a complicated-sounding computer system in a call centre slash electronics factory, and he'd taken the opportunity to travel a bit. He told us in great detail all the things he'd seen over there—beaches, islands, a vegan festival where he'd tasted a bunch of new fruit and vegetables, a secluded monastery where he'd meditated in the country's northern mountains—and even though it was fascinating and all, I couldn't manage to show any enthusiasm. I nodded a few times and asked one or two questions so I wouldn't look like I was bored to death. On the way home, I asked Saké how I'd done.

"With what?" she asked.

"The conversations, tonight in general."

"What? Didn't you have fun?"

"I did. But usually I don't do so well in that kind of social setting, especially not with people I just met."

"It's all good. I didn't notice a thing."

We walked quietly for a while.

"So you don't go out a lot, eh?"

"Meh."

I waited a few minutes before explaining.

"I have friends, I go out a little, but most of the time I'd rather be alone."

"Are you kidding? We used to get along so damned well!"

"I know, but we haven't seen each other in a long time. I just forgot how, I guess."

Soon we were back in front of our building. Saké had only been living with us for a day, but it felt like she'd been there forever. That was how she acted anyway. She unlocked the door to the apartment using the key my dad had had cut for her earlier that day.

"I really liked Rajani, and Arnaud's nice, too."

"Yeah, they're cool... Goodnight now!" she said, slamming her bedroom door.

I did the same. I lay down on my bed still wearing my clothes and put a Joni Mitchell album on the old record player my dad had given me a few years before, along with his whole record collection. I grabbed the book from my bedside table. Mitchell's biography, where I'd read that she'd dated Leonard Cohen for a while. I focused on the part about how *A Case of You* came to be, and I listened to it three or four times over. I knew I was going to be obsessed with it now for the next few weeks. I like sad stories, ones filled with sorrow.

Hollywood

UNDERGROUND POEM #3

like elevator music
to kill time
and since dreams are forever the same
I will sing like a poorly tuned piano
so as to keep the night and
hotel rooms company

After the sandman

THEY BOTH TAKE HOURS TO FALL ASLEEP, except when they use chemicals to hurry things along. Then they meet, one lying down, the other sitting at the foot of the bed. The thick curtains let just a chink of light filter through, a bluish glow that cloaks the furniture, even more nondescript in the dark, bags lying open every which way, the impersonal prints against the wallpaper often dreadful, even in the most luxurious hotels. One talks about a movie he's seen a thousand times, and the other about a record he's just picked up at a second-hand store. They are motionless, or nearly. Their relationship is intellectual, no need to use their bodies. They know it won't last, that day will come to replace night and they'll both disappear, but they also know that they will meet again at nightfall, perhaps in the same place, perhaps in another room, in another hotel, what difference does it make?

If they both got up to part the curtains and look out the window, even the city lights wouldn't stop them seeing that outside the sky is raging and the stars are flying past each other at breakneck speed, trailing clouds of extraterrestrial dust in their wake.

Xavier

I WOKE UP IN THE MIDDLE OF THE NIGHT, like every night, and made my way to the bathroom to drink some water. I'd caught a chill from walking in the storm and now my throat was tight and I had trouble swallowing. I washed a few pills down with water, company samples, whatever was handy. Just like every night for some time now. It didn't bother me that my sore throat might affect my work the next day. I just wanted to get back to sleep. Get back to my dream.

The TV clicked on at six in the morning: these days guests no longer wake up to the sound of the phone ringing, but to France 2 or some other channel from the TV menu. I stretched for a while in the bed, which was so comfortable I had trouble resigning myself to getting up. After belting out a loud yawn to rouse myself, I turned my attention to what was on TV. A woman standing in front of a satellite map streaked with different colours was explaining the weather outside.

"...caused by a depression of unheard dimensions. Atmospheric pressure adjusted to sea level is moving horizontally towards a mass of low pressure somewhere in the Atlantic off the coast of Greenland. What we see here is a mass of freezing-cold air. It has the centre of our area of low pressure surrounded, covering a radius of over two thousand kilometres."

The camera switched back to the studio and focused on the host, who seemed a bit lost.

"But what does all that mean for the man and woman on the street, Paloma?"

"What does it mean? It means that the snowfall will continue for several days to come. It also means we won't be able to predict what will happen next. A second mass of low pressure appears to be forming near Canada, and with what we know today, it's not too early to think it could hit France in a few days. But we're keeping a close eye on the first mass of low pressure that's affecting us right now. Laurent, it's difficult to talk about this storm in rational, scientific terms. There's just no explaining low pressure on this scale."

"Paloma, tell us what's going on in America."

I got up and raised the volume to listen to the report while I washed up.

"Things aren't as bad in North America as they are here, Laurent. In Canada, snowfall recorded so far is still under the record levels of 1999. And the authorities are well equipped to handle this type of low-pressure system. Constant snowfall, not volume, is what complicates snow removal. But things are much more chaotic in the United States. Annual municipal budgets for snow removal have been wiped out in two days. Public works departments are too understaffed to cope, and cities don't have enough equipment. Luckily, the storm has only hit the East Coast. Reinforcements from the Midwest, from Chicago, Indianapolis and Columbus, are on their way to help local authorities. The situation is even more disastrous here in Europe. France, Belgium, the Netherlands, Germany and parts of the UK have been completely paralyzed. The death toll is rising by the hour, Laurent. People are stuck in their cars; many have gone missing. Spain and Portugal have not been the hardest hit by the snowfall, but they have suffered the most damage. We're talking about an unprecedented situation in both countries, and their governments have already declared a state of emergency. It goes without saying that domestic and international flights have been cancelled. Trains are still in operation, but there are significant delays."

"Thank you, Paloma..."

I turned off the TV. The door opened and Antony barged into the room.

"Dude. *T'es prêt?*"

"Yeah, give me a minute."

I slipped on my shoes, not bothering to lace them up.

"I'll need to come back up after breakfast. You know where the appointment is?"

"Kensington Suite. First floor. There'll be ten of them or so, so I guess it will be 'boardroom style.' OK, you coming?"

"One last thing."

I bent down to open the minibar. I hesitated for a second, then opted for a small bottle of vodka that I knocked back in two gulps.

"Xavier, shit... even I wouldn't have the balls!"

"Well, my dear friend," I replied. "I really need it this morning."

I cleared my throat, coughed a little, then took the key card from the nightstand and pushed Antony back out of the room. I was hungry.

"Do you have a ritual for when you get to a hotel?"

"A ritual?"

"Things you do to settle in."

Antony took a bite of bread.

"*Non, pas vraiment*," he said, his mouth full. "Except maybe turning on the TV and seeing what channels they have."

I gulped down a strawberry, barely chewing it.

"You?"

"Usually, yeah."

"And the problem is...?"

I laughed.

"There is no problem."

"Xavier, fuck. I know you. You're asking because something's up."

I meant to take a sip of coffee, but Antony put his hand on my cup.

"Xavier, get it off your chest."

"I usually have a little routine when I walk into the room: I pull back the sheets, open the curtains, turn on all the lights if it's dark outside, rummage through the closets and look in all the drawers. It's like I need to get to know my surroundings before I can feel comfortable. But when I checked in here, I sat down to watch a movie right away and didn't think twice about any of it. Not at all. It completely slipped my mind. And nothing happened."

"If nothing happened, why are you complaining?"

"I'm not complaining. I just hope it doesn't mean that I've gotten used to living in places that aren't really me."

"Are you going to finish your eggs?"

"No, you can have them."

I pushed my plate across the table.

::

It was Antony who sold it. Not me. Even though we'll both get the same commission on the spectacular sale he managed to pull off. I talked a bit, presented some charts, vaguely tried to be convincing, but I really didn't do much.

At the hotel bar where Antony insisted on celebrating, our phones both beeped at the same time: a message from Pullman, sending us e-tickets for a ferry that evening

43

from Portsmouth to Bilbao, a trip that would take thirty-three hours and forty-five minutes.

"No fucking way."

I ordered another drink. Antony glared at me.

"We've got ten minutes to get our things together. Pullman even called a taxi for us."

"It won't take me ten minutes to have another drink. And shit, he really wants us to go to Bilbao... How much do you want to bet the convention's been cancelled?"

The server arrived with a whiskey. I threw back half the glass. I winced. I didn't much like whiskey, but only a drink like this would do in the circumstances: a strong amber that cleansed and burned on its way down.

"If the convention were cancelled, Pullman wouldn't have paid for a taxi to Portsmouth. That can't have been cheap in shitty weather like this."

My phone went off again. A call this time. I answered.

"Xavier Adam."

"Adam, it's Pullman."

I turned towards Antony.

"It's Pullman. How much do you want to bet?"

"Stop fooling around and talk to him. I want to know why he's calling."

"Mr. Pullman, yes, how are you?"

"Good, good. Listen: the taxi company called me. They say they only have one guy willing to drive you to Portsmouth and he wants to leave right now. So get your things at once, he's waiting for you outside. He's charging me a fortune so you better not make him wait."

Pullman hung up before I could say anything. I gave Antony the good news. We went up to our rooms to pack.

Up there, as if to redeem myself, I threw back the bedcovers, opened the curtains and the window, too, turned on the TV and all the lights. I took a few bottles from the minibar and threw them into my suitcase along with the clothes littering the floor. I went through the room a couple of times, opening all the drawers, checking under the bed, in the closets. I hadn't forgotten anything. Antony came in. I offered him the bottle of vodka I'd put away in my jacket pocket. *"Pourquoi pas?"* he said, taking it.

"My suitcase is full of them."

"Mine too."

We handed our keys to the desk clerk, who pointed to the car waiting for us on the other side of the revolving doors and explained that the motorways had been cleared and the snow had turned to a drizzle.

"You're lucky! Have a safe trip to Portsmouth, gentlemen."

I thanked him, but I felt like groaning. I was sure the drive would be every bit as awful as the ferry to Bilbao. Luckily Pullman had booked us a cabin. I'd be able to put back a few drinks and get some sleep. I checked the reservation after settling into the back seat of the taxi, which started moving before we'd closed the door.

"We'll be sharing a bunk, you and me."

"Quoi? You can't be serious. Let me take a look at this shit."

Antony made a grab for my phone, only to realize it wasn't true. My idea of a joke, just to annoy him. I opened my bag and picked out two small bottles of Dubonnet vermouth. I handed him one.

"Here. To calm you down."

"Well," he said, cracking open the bottle. "To the two bunks in our cabin. Cheers!"

"Cheers!"

He threw my phone onto the seat. The taxi driver turned up the radio. It would be a long ride.

But somewhere, between two songs I didn't know, a reggae number with hip-hop undertones aroused some inner demon: I wanted to cry like a baby. Scary chills popped up all over my body; I was covered in goose bumps and big fat tears rolled down my cheeks. Yeah, I'd made a mess of my life. I turned towards the window to hide my distress from Antony. The rain had turned back into snow. We could barely see the cars coming in the opposite direction, which didn't stop the driver heading full-speed into the blizzard. My stomach hurt. I leaned my forehead against the frozen window and closed my eyes. It was starting again. I counted to ten...

We arrived at the Portsmouth waterfront in less than two hours. A ferry was leaving for Le Havre, bursting at the seams. For the time being it was just about the only way to get to Paris, other than the Channel Tunnel. Our boat was docked casually to one side. Antony thanked the taxi driver and we headed over to the loading platform. Just as I stepped onto the boat, it crossed my mind that I might die in a storm while crossing the English Channel. Everything was out of my hands: where I went, how I spent my time, what I wanted, right down to when I would die. I was delighted by the prospect. We found our cabin. I dropped my bags onto the bottom berth.

Xavier

Feeling alienated from the rest of the world. Also, a need to examine the existence I keep doubting. Often, I close a book or turn off the TV and think: that's it, that's exactly it. And I have no one to talk to about any of this. Other than that weird guy who visits me in my dreams.

"Hollywood," he told me when I asked his name. Who calls their kid Hollywood? "My parents," he replied. He asked if we were in my dream or his. It's my hotel room, so it must be my dream. Then I woke up.

Reality is harnessed through language. I read or heard that somewhere. And it seems disarmingly obvious. If I don't put my inability to live into words, it will never be harnessed. This is how a child learns to name things, to appropriate them. I spend long periods thinking and struggling a bit and it seems I like it, this state of unhealthy melancholy. And then there are the dreams.

Hollywood

I WAS SWEEPING the paved footpath between the grave-stones when I noticed that the beans I'd planted only a couple of days before had already started to sprout. All of a sudden, I felt lost, as if I were a stranger to everything around me. I could see the thin green stalks poking through the ground before the grave of Joseph-Elzéar Masson, who died in 1934, and the sun setting in the distance, and the pink clouds resting on the horizon. I saw it all, but none of it, or almost none of it, felt familiar. The feeling lasted a few seconds, a minute at most, and I recovered just as quickly. I thought: beans, what a funny idea! Anyway... I went back to sweeping the path. I brushed away a few stones and moved on.

I took the bus home. Dusk was deepening into night: blinds had been drawn, so you couldn't see inside townhouses or apartments anymore. Street lights flooded the pavement with an orange hue, and the sky was growing darker and darker; you could almost see the saturation as blue turned into black. I had a sudden craving for ice cream, so I got off the bus and walked to the dairy parlour close to home. I ordered a vanilla cone dipped in milk chocolate, which I savoured slowly as I baby-stepped my way home. I wasn't in a hurry, even though it was hot out. I've always liked feeling hot.

I barely had time to open the apartment door before Saké pushed me right back out.

"You're coming with me."

"What? Wait..."

I resisted: I wanted to at least get changed. My clothes were dusty and there was sand in my shoes.

"Hurry up," she said. "The auditions are in less than an hour."

I wanted to ask her: auditions for what? But instead I ran to my room to change. I'd have time to squeeze some info out of her once we were out of the apartment. Saké was already losing patience.

"Chop chop, Holly."

"Coming!" I yelled from my room.

She was standing on the landing with her hand on the knob, ready to close the door. I went out half-naked. I tried to put my shirt on as I was going out the door, but I got my head stuck in one of the sleeves. I was literally in a tight spot. Saké sighed.

"Are you fucking kidding me?"

50

She helped me put my shirt on properly. We ran down the five flights of stairs to the street. Once on the sidewalk, I started grilling her.

"So, where are we going exactly?"

"I told you: auditions. In less than an hour. We have to hurry, I don't want to miss the show."

"Auditions for what?"

"You'll see."

"What the fuck, Saké... Just tell me!"

"If I tell you, you'll just run out on me and go home."

I pretended to turn around and leave; Saké grabbed me by the arm.

"Hollywood, you're coming with me!"

Resistance was futile, I knew it. We turned the corner as a bus was passing by. Saké started running, still clutching my arm. The bus stopped and waited for us. We walked all the way to the back and sat down, even though the bus was empty.

"Is this for one of your hair show things?" I asked.

"No. I told them about you and they're interested, but they said they wouldn't be holding more casting sessions before the summer. I mean... before June. I'll get back to you later on that."

She stayed quiet for a few minutes before she went on: "Now, you have to promise you'll at least give it a try."

"How can I promise when I don't know where you're dragging me off to?"

"Oh come on, say yes. Do it for me."

"I suck at acting, Saké. You want me to promise to make a fool of myself in public."

"It's not for a play. You really think they'd be holding auditions at 11 p.m.?"

"How should I know? I don't know anything about that stuff."

Saké turned to look out the window.

A couple of stops further, she started giggling.

"What kind of underwear do you have on tonight? Briefs? Boxers?"

"Er... Why do you want to know?"

She got up.

"No reason. Come on: this is our stop."

The bus let us off. To our right, a massive parking lot engulfed a tiny mall, a bowling alley, a bar and an exotic grocery store. Saké led me across the lot to the bar. We stopped on the nearly empty terrace. It said on the poster that the auditions were at 11 p.m., but not what they were for. I understood straight away.

"No. No way. No way. You're crazy, Saké!"

"Oh come on, it'll be fun! Plus you'll love the song I picked out for you."

"What? You put a number together?"

She burst out laughing.

"Not a number, no. I went through your stuff and brought a CD from your collection. All you have to do is dance. Improvise. It'll be fun!"

"What did you pick?"

"I didn't look very long. I just took one of the CDs on your bedside table."

"Which one?"

Saké pulled up a chair and sank into it. She opened her bag and took her cigarettes out, bringing one to her lips before handing me the pack. I said no.

"Come on, tell me which one you picked."

She lit a cigarette and inhaled deeply before fishing the CD out of her bag. She put it on the table.

"You're absolutely nuts if you think I'm gonna dance naked to Leonard Cohen!"

"But you can't say no. This album is the bomb!"

"I know it's great. But what in the world were you thinking? Nobody in their right mind would dance naked to Leonard Cohen. Not in a bar, anyway. Especially not a gay bar."

"OK, granted, the first few songs may not be appropriate, but I'm sure you'll do just fine with the one I picked."

For the moment, the music debate prevented me from seeing how absurd the whole thing was. I asked Saké what song she chose.

"*I'm Your Man.* It's totally hot. I can picture you slowly taking off your clothes to the song, piece by piece. The man's voice is so sexy. Plus it's the perfect song. I mean, I don't know him much—Leonard Cohen's your thing—you know I don't usually listen to that kind of stuff. But ever since you made me listen to this CD, don't ask me why, I'm sort of obsessed with it. It somehow got inside my head, as if it was urging me to do something with it. So I thought about it long and hard. And earlier this week, I came to eat at that Chinese place next door and saw the audition poster, and it suddenly dawned on me: I knew I had to make you dance naked to *I'm Your Man*. It felt like this was precisely what the song had wanted all along."

"Fuck, Saké. You are batshit crazy..."

I had nothing to add. No arguments. I had neither the strength nor the conviction to sway her. I sat down on a chair and took a cigarette from the pack she'd left on the table. I leaned over and she struck a match for me.

"What about you? Are you in the show?" I asked.

"No. I'm not a guy! I'm your manager."

"My manager?"

I sighed.

"And you've pictured me dancing naked?"

"Well... not that way, you know that."

I had to prove I was over eighteen before I was allowed backstage.

"I'm sorry, miss, but women aren't allowed in here."

Saké gave me a peck on the cheek.

"Good luck! I'll go and give your CD to the sound technician. See you after your number! You're on third."

I had no time to react. Saké pushed me into the dressing room and the bouncer closed the door behind me.

The room was big and full of guys, most of whom were buff, stripped to the waist, oiled up and checking themselves out in one of the mirrors that covered the walls. Some were lifting weights or doing push-ups, bulking up for the moment of truth. Guys dressed up as firemen, policemen, vampires or construction workers; or warming up, busting a few dance moves, stretching this way and that. I sat down on the first chair I could find, a cramp ripping through my chest. A caller came to tell us the auditions would start in five. I thought: OK, I'm here, I'll do it, I won't choke. I breathed deeply and the cramp subsided. I must have looked lost in my cotton t-shirt and jeans, a look that screamed "I'm-just-this-regular-guy-who-doesn't-feel-too-good." A stripper dressed as a computer technician or whatever asked me if I needed help.

"Actually, I don't have a costume. I'm not ready for this at all."

He pointed to a closet at the back of the room.

"You'll find all kinds of things in there. And if that doesn't work out, I could let you wear my fireman outfit. I wasn't sure whether to go with that or the one I'm wearing, but since three other guys are already going as firemen, I picked this one."

"Thanks, that's nice, but I'd rather go for something else too. Er... and what are you supposed to be, exactly?"

"A nerd. Geek is the new sexy, dude."

"Oh. I didn't know."

I got up and thanked him for his help. I took a moment to go through the costumes hanging in the closet. All the uniforms were there: policeman, soldier, gendarme, sailor, you name it. The famous Chippendale collar and bow tie. A cape. Wigs. Nothing very Leonard Cohen there, if such a thing were even possible. I picked a suit and tie that didn't fit me quite right. All eyes turned on me as I undressed. The nerd with the big glasses rushed to my rescue.

"You won't be dancing in those boxers, I hope?"

"Er... I don't know. Yes? No?"

"No. They're way too loose. You need a G-string or a jockstrap. Or at least briefs."

He showed me what he was wearing under his black pants. I didn't quite know what I was meant to say.

"Actually, they're all I have. I didn't bring anything else."

"OK, wait a sec."

He turned to the other strippers, who were all staring at me.

"Could someone lend a jockstrap or a pair of tighty-whities to our friend here?"

A whisper went through the crowd. A guy dressed as a vampire threw my new ally a jockstrap. I took off my boxer shorts and put on the thing he was brandishing—somebody else's underwear. I got dressed. My new friend helped me put on the tie. The caller came in.

"Guys, it's showtime!" he said, before he looked over his notes. "Hmm... Joey Moretti."

A lifeguard sporting huge sunglasses and a lifebelt followed the caller out of the dressing room. The nerd asked me if I knew when I was up.

"I'm third. You?"

"Second. And what are you dancing to?"

We could hear the music through the backstage door. Hip hop with lewd, explicit lyrics. Obviously. I felt ashamed.

"Leonard Cohen," I confessed, quietly.

"Um. Never heard of him. I picked a song by Peaches: *Fuck the Pain Away*."

"Er... Cool."

The music stopped. We could hear the audience cheering. Each performance was graded by three judges from the bar, as well as the level of applause. The lifeguard came back into the dressing room: he was naked, hard and gleaming with sweat. My new friend kissed me on the mouth and ran to catch up with the caller. I sat down on a bench near the door and waited my turn. The vampire who'd lent me his underwear was pacing up and down.

The audience applauded. I was up.

From the very first notes, I knew I wouldn't get much applause. I loosened my tie without moving the rest of my body. I didn't know what else to do. Someone at the bar cleared their throat. From sheer discomfort, most likely. I was blinded by the harsh spotlights, but I spotted Saké, her face, her hands; she was waving at me, trying to tell me something. Swaying my hips, I took off the oversized jacket and threw it into the crowd. Nothing. Maybe throwing your clothes into the crowd wasn't in anymore. I undid my shirt in a way that was meant to be hot to go with Leonard Cohen's sexy voice, but I couldn't work the magic: the last button wouldn't budge, so I had to pull the shirt up and over my head to take it off. I turned around to unzip my pants, letting them down slowly as I kept on dancing, but there was zero reaction when the audience caught sight of my ass. I let my pants fall down to my ankles and tried to kick them off, but I tripped as I turned to face the crowd, falling flat on my face. Someone let out a yelp. A few people coughed. Saké cracked up.

I was hoping the technician would stop the music on compassionate grounds but he must have been laughing his ass off, too. So I tried to pass it off as a dance move. I wriggled my way across the floor, face down, like a porn star in a low-budget flick. Then I got up and lowered the jockstrap, revealing my pubes. Problem was I didn't have a hard-on. I've never been to a strip show myself, but I'm pretty sure they give you more than the sorry sight of a limp dick. I just stood there, stock still. I let the underwear fall to the ground. I cupped myself instinctively, only to realize that this was exactly what I wasn't supposed to do. I put my hands on my hips and swayed them some more, not knowing what else I could do. The song was almost over anyway.

No one clapped. I picked up my clothes and walked back to the dressing room.

Saké was laughing so hard she cried.

Hollywood

UNDERGROUND POEM #5

the day breaks like a jackhammer
with concrete dust
learning to count backwards should be a must
when you tell me about all the films I have yet to see

After the sandman

THEY FEEL AS THOUGH, as with each time they meet, nothing exists apart from this room bathed in a bluish light. They talk in hushed voices of their humiliations. They are blasé and beautiful.

Then the window is shattered and the weighty curtain torn away. A pebble no bigger than a penny bounces onto the worn carpet, leaving a dark imprint. Hollywood bends over to pick up the object that has fallen to Earth. The stone is scorching hot; he throws it onto the bed. Xavier picks it up in turn and immediately drops it onto the quilt; it's still too hot to handle. They walk over to the window, avoiding the shards of glass that litter the floor.

One by one, the stars are falling from the sky.

Xavier

ANTONY WANTED TO CELEBRATE OUR SUCCESS, and since I rarely turn down an invitation to drink, I joined him. We emptied all the little bottles he had thrown into his suitcase, then we attacked those I'd brought with me. Vodka, gin, rum and scotch, of course, as well as Brandy Special Reserve, Chambord Liqueur Royale de France, El Grito Blue Agave Tequila, Old Charter Bourbon, Midori Melon Liqueur and Jack Daniel's Tennessee Whiskey. Obviously, I was sick. Antony too. The ferry pitched dangerously from the wind, the waves and the storm that was pelting down on the English Channel—on the entire world, really. Luckily, our Club cabin that overlooked the furious waters came with a shower and toilet. I washed up after I vomited all over myself, then took a few pills from Antony's bag: a drug for severe nausea prescribed for cancer patients on chemo. I fell into a dreamless sleep for a good ten hours. When I finally woke up, Antony was sitting on the top berth eating melon and strawberries.

"There's fresh fruit in a basket just over there. And, of course, a minibar!"

He threw me a bunch of grapes that I gobbled down. I looked through the cabin porthole. Torrents of black water were pounding against the thick glass. It was almost impossible to see anything. It was warm in the cabin. I felt pretty good.

"What time is it?" I asked.

"I have no fuckin' clue. It's dark, maybe it's night. My phone is on the counter, just over there."

"It doesn't matter. I'd rather not know. Toss me something else, I'm hungry."

I caught a banana, which I devoured.

"I'm going to see what the restaurant has to eat. You want something?"

"*Non, c'est bon*. I ate too much fruit. I'll have to take a shit soon."

I got dressed and went out. I eyed the upscale Four Seasons menu for a moment, but then thought better of it. The restaurant was closed anyway. I opted instead for a pastry, a sandwich and a bottle of sparkling water from a small café that was still open. There was only one customer, an old man who asked me if I knew which band was playing at the Sunset Show Bar the following day. I stared at him for a moment; he was a typical vacationer: sweatshirt, jeans, ugly walking shoes, more concerned with enjoying himself than with the seconds ticking away, everything he had to do and all the rest of it. He wanted to listen to live music and sip his bourbon, while the sea tore itself apart and the sky fell in on our heads and we might all die, shipwrecked on the ferry that had dared to cross the Channel and part of the Atlantic when doomsday arrived. I got up and left the café. The alcohol and drugs had evidently affected me: here I was getting all worked up about the end of the world and my imminent death. I thought back to how I felt when I stepped onto the boat. I had to recover the nonchalance that had worked so well for me in the past.

I took a walk around the ship. I stopped by the hair salon, where the stylist was waiting patiently for the night to end and the day to begin. He couldn't sleep in this weather, he explained, as he gave me a ridiculously overpriced cut. He almost did permanent damage, twice coming close to puncturing an eye as the waves knocked the ferry about. I passed by a spa that didn't open until nine o'clock, then a small casino where I lost two hundred dollars at roulette. I went back to the cabin. Antony was sleeping. I checked the time: 5:13 a.m. I got undressed, took a sleeping pill and fell asleep instantly.

I woke up a little after noon. I felt queasy: drugs and alcohol and erratic sleep and seasickness. Antony wanted to eat at the Four Seasons. I said no thanks. I stayed back and made myself black tea. The boat lurched violently and I spilled the piping-hot liquid all over my lap. I screamed. Someone knocked on the door.

"Is everything all right?"

I opened the door just enough to see a young woman who had been passing by and heard me yell.

"Yes, I'm OK. I burned myself with a hot cup of tea."

"OK then. Have a nice day, sir. And be careful."

I watched her walk away, then closed the door. I cleaned up the mess, sat on the floor of the shower and let the water run over my head until Antony walked in to tell me all about his meal and how the waitress with a perfect ass had made eyes at him while he waited at the bar for a table.

We pulled into Santurtzi a little after 7 p.m. I wanted to take the metro, but Antony insisted we hail a cab, even though he knew the roads would be blocked. An hour later we arrived at the Abba Parque Hotel. We ate in the hotel restaurant, the Botavara, and then I went straight to my room to hide. I lay down on the bed without closing my eyes, and though I didn't sleep a wink, I didn't get up until the next morning.

The snow hadn't stopped. In the lobby and over breakfast, the hotel guests spoke only of the weather. I'd had enough. I went out to explore the city. It wasn't as cold or as damp as London. The gently falling snow made me think of Toronto, or those movies set in New York in the winter—which were probably shot in Toronto. An innocent snow, pretty enough if you like winter, almost romantic even. But Bilbao isn't able to deal with wintry conditions like Toronto, it isn't a movie set: the streets were deserted, people didn't dare take their cars out. Grocery stores had been practically raided in the early hours of the storm, and since shipments and deliveries were taking longer than usual to arrive, whole shelves were empty, or nearly. Restaurants that had stayed open were making a killing. And the clubs, the last bastions against the mass hysteria that threatened to descend upon the human race, were packed.

I walked into a tiny bar. It seemed fine: the speakers weren't blaring the latest big hit. There was almost no one inside. A woman was talking to the server over by the bar. In front of a mirror, two people were dancing to oldies the manager had probably dusted off just for them. Posters on the walls advertising a rock concert that evening had been slapped with "SUSPENDIDO" printed in bold black letters across a red banner. *Debido a la tormenta de nieve*, the server came over and told me. I ordered a rum & coke, local style:

"*Un cuba libre, por favor.*"

"*¡Inmediatamente, señor!*" he replied, walking away.

I sat by the door, my back to the wall, to get a better look at the locals. People came in, and the music got louder as the cloud of cigarette smoke thickened. Around 1 a.m. I got up to dance. I'd had a lot to drink and gorged myself on tapas and *papas fritas*. I'd been in the bar for over ten hours. I was on the brink of euphoria, a quiet, syrupy, almost sensual euphoria. The bar was packed by now. I couldn't dance to the music—it was too strange—but I let myself go, swaying any which way. People smiled at me, everyone was dancing in their own haphazard fashion. I'd chosen the right place, it seemed, to improvise.

When I got too hot I left, leaving my coat lying on the table. I needed to cool down a bit. I walked out with a glass of red wine and a cigarette, courtesy of a server. The snow was still falling, just as slow and heavy as before. I suddenly wanted to find a kitchenware store to buy a pie dish and whip up decadent desserts. It felt like Christmas. I leaned up against the old stone wall and took a drag on my cigarette, lazily exhaling the smoke like they do in the movies. I threw the butt into the snow, left my glass on the ground and turned down the snowy backstreet. I walked for a while, zigzagging through the narrow lanes of the Casco Viejo. I listened to the snow crunch under my feet and I ran my fingertips along the old stone walls. I was on the verge of tears, prompted both by happiness at seeing so much snow and the vacuity of my pitiful existence. Then a howl pulled me from my reverie. A howl of pain. I ran towards the sound.

"*¡Ayúdame por favor, alguien!* Help!"

I turned a corner and came across a woman sitting in the snow, legs splayed and skirt hitched up, her eyes full of tears, her face red and sweaty. Blood had stained the snow beside her. It didn't take me long to put two and two together: she was in labour.

"Fuck, shit! Uh... *No hablo español muy bien. ¿Habla francés?* Do you speak French? English?"

She answered between howls in French with English undertones, but with softer consonants and a guttural accent.

"Oui. S'il vous plaît, aidez-moi. I don't want my baby to be born in a pile of snow."

She started to laugh and tears rolled down her cheeks. I searched through my pockets but couldn't find my phone. I must have left it in my coat back at the bar.

"I'll go find a taxi or an ambulance. Don't move."

"Where could I go like this?"

She burst out laughing, but a contraction caught her unawares. She buried her face in her hands and let out a scream. I started to run. I turned the corner and ended up at the foot of the cathedral. No one was there. I took a left, then another left. I passed the bar. I went in to grab my coat and phone and dialled 112, trying to retrace my steps without getting lost. In a mixture of English, basic Spanish and very crude Basque, I told the man on the other end of the line where to find us.

"Artekale numéro treinta y uno. In front of the Ziba dress store."

Minutes later, an ambulance arrived. Two paramedics got out, shouting something in Basque. They helped the woman get to her feet and climb into the vehicle. I followed them in. One of them closed the door behind me, and the ambulance started off towards the nearest hospital.

"¿Es usted el padre?"

"In English, please..."

"Are you the father?"

I said no, and they wouldn't let me into the room with Gia. Gia Kasapi is what she told the triage nurse who had asked her name. She got out her papers: an Albanian passport, a Canadian passport and a Quebec health insurance card. I've lived in Montreal, she said, seeing the surprise on my face, since the Kosovo War.

I waited until someone came to get me, less than thirty minutes later.

"It was a fast delivery. The baby was crowning. You did well bringing her to the hospital. Now both of them are safe and healthy."

I thanked the doctor and went into the room. Gia was exhausted; her eyes were swollen, her cheeks red, her hair a mess.

"I won't stay long, I just wanted to make sure everything was OK."

"Yes, thanks. It was very nice of you to come along. I'm sorry to have put you through all this."

I smiled. "It wasn't a problem."

She closed her eyes for a moment, then smiled back at me.

"Thank you. I'd like to get some sleep. Could you come back tomorrow? I wouldn't mind some company."

"Tomorrow, as in, in a few hours?"

Gia smiled.

"Say, tomorrow evening?"

"I've got a conference in the afternoon. I'll skip the cocktail and come see you."

"Thank you, Xavier. See you soon."

I said goodbye and left the room. I looked at my phone: 5:36 a.m. I walked to San Mamés metro station, which didn't open until six. I read a newspaper that someone had left behind while I waited, then I took the first train. I got off at Casco Viejo station, because I knew how to get back to the hotel from there. I retraced my steps from the day before. It was barely snowing; maybe the storm was finally over. I walked for about twenty minutes, then turned right onto avenida Sabino Arana. To my left I saw San Mamés station, which turned out to be right beside the hotel. I sighed and turned right onto Rodriguez Arias Kalea. I pushed open the lobby door and went up to my room, dragging my feet. It was almost 7 a.m.

In the stairwell, I realized I hadn't introduced myself to Gia. How did she know my name? I slid the key card across the magnetic strip in the lock at least twenty times without any luck. She'd called me by my first name... The door swung open and Antony was standing in the frame in his underwear, his hair a mess of tangles.

"Xavier? What are you doing?"

"Oh sorry, wrong room." I walked to the next door. My key worked on the first try. I nodded at Antony before closing the door behind me. There was a knock right away.

"You just got in?"

"Yeah. I'm going to sleep. I'm tired."

I wanted to close the door, but Antony came into the room. He didn't appear to be in a good mood.

"No shit you're tired! It's seven fuckin' o'clock. We've got a pitch in six hours, man."

"I know, which is why I'm going to bed."

He stretched, then looked me right in the eyes.

"You won't pull the same shit as in London, will you? I know I can do the job by myself, but I don't have a partner for nothing. Xavier, shit, what's going on?"

"Relax, Antony. I'll sleep a little, take a cold shower, and the pitch will be fine. It's my product, I know it by heart."

"You know, Pullman called about London and I didn't tell on you... Don't make me change my mind and call him back."

"Go back to bed, Antony."

I pushed him out into the hallway and closed the door.

I hadn't fallen asleep without pills or alcohol for a long time. It was strange when I woke up: I felt great, even though I'd only slept two or three hours. I dressed quickly and went downstairs to eat in a little café. A blazing sun shone in a cloudless sky. The snow was melting slowly and barely dressed children were throwing snowballs and shouting. The storm was over. I would be able to go back to Toronto. I sent Antony a message asking him to meet me in my room an hour before the pitch. Then I sat down with an orange pekoe and a *pan tostado con tomate y queso* and pretended to read the newspaper; I hardly understood a word and didn't much want to know what was going on in the world.

"Did you knot your tie yourself or did you ask your daddy?"

"Fuck, man, what's your problem? This is the way I always tie it!"

"Yo, Xavier, *calme-toi!*"

Antony tossed his leather briefcase onto the bed, laughing.

"Come here, I'll fix it for you."

He undid my tie, turned up my collar and slid the jacket down my shoulders. I felt like he was going to undress me, as if we were rehearsing a love scene for a B movie.

"Have you ever kissed a guy?" I asked him.

He stopped tying and took a step back.

"*Quoi?*"

I looked at him without saying a word. He stared at me, then went back to the tie. He tied it tight and I pretended to choke. Antony turned down my collar, pulled up my jacket and brushed his hands across my shoulders as though to be sure no dust would disgrace the immaculate black. He gave the lapels a quick tug as a finishing touch and took another step back.

"There, that's better."

He picked up his briefcase.

"If that's what's bothering you, Xavier, it's not the end of the world. My sister knows a lot of people, I could ask her to set you up with a good-looking rich dude."

I burst out laughing.

"Don't worry about it. I'm not gay. I just don't know what to do with my life and I thought maybe..."

"You thought that kissing a guy would change something? And you want to kiss me?"

"Not you, necessarily. Oh, forget it."

"Yeah! *Bonne idée...*"

We left the room. The conference was less than five hundred metres from the hotel, in the Palacio de Congresos Euskalduna. We walked over. The melting snow slowed us down, since we had to avoid the puddles and mud. We got to the Palacio in less than ten minutes. Our meeting with the leading experts from the Colegio Oficial de Médicos de Bizkaia was in room D3.

This time, I pulled off the sale. With Antony's help, of course.

Xavier

Dreaming is our way of fleeing—reality, and everything else. We flee because we aren't comfortable anywhere and we want to see if things might be better someplace else. And because we need to believe in something. Something beautiful. Even if we know nothing is real.

If only life could be a burst of fireworks or a meteor shower, like in my dreams. Is it because the storm is over that I suddenly feel lighter, less empty? Or is it because of Gia?

When I finally close my eyes, the dream picks up where it left off. As if whole days were nothing but short breaks. Even if we don't always meet up in the same place. There is a seemingly indistinguishable boundary that can nevertheless be perceived by the mind: sleep. Beyond this, though, I cannot comment on what possibly or probably

happens while we're awake or asleep. How can we under-
stand what we never witness? I have only memories of
my dreams, memories unrelated to any "real" event, but
which are just as true as the fact that I exist.

Hollywood

"HOLLYWOOD! I just got a letter and some cash from my parents. *You* are coming shopping!"

She shut the door as fast as she'd opened it. I got up and put on my socks and shoes. Saké was waiting in the lobby.

"Did they tell you where they are?"

"Who?"

"Your parents."

"Oh, them... Nope. Take a look for yourself."

She handed me the letter.

Saké. We hope you are well. We are thinking of you. Here's a little money for you. Please say hello to everyone for us.

"That's it?"

"Yup."

"Doesn't it bother you?"

"What?"

"That they're not telling you more, as if they'd just gone off on vacation?"

"You think they went off on vacation?"

"No, that's not what I meant."

Saké took my head in both hands.

"Yo, Hollywood, listen to me: I don't know where my folks are and it really doesn't bother me. I'm not in denial, I know it's sad and all, but I'm not upset. I'm totally OK with the fact that I may never see them again. So stop it already: don't worry for me or try to push feelings onto me. *This* is my reaction: we're going shopping!"

She dragged me into the first store we came across. Luckily, it was a second-hand store, and a decent one at that. We could've landed just as easily in a medical supplies outlet or a health food store.

"Get whatever you like. I'm paying," she said, tossing me a bunch of clothes to try on: a denim jacket, a pair of corduroy pants, a flower print shirt, a long skirt and a few wigs.

"I'm not a doll, Saké."

"Oh come on, we're just having fun. Plus I think you should dress a little more... fierce."

"Like wearing-a-skirt fierce? No thank you!"

"OK, I'll drop the skirt. But try on the rest."

I did what I was told. I locked myself into a fitting room and started catwalking for Saké, who giggled when she saw me in the denim jacket. She insisted on buying me the flower print shirt. She bought herself a couple of wigs, a few pairs of jeans and leggings, a bunch of shoes and close to a dozen handbags. The salesgirl smiled when we got to the cash register. She was having a good day: Saké had just bought three hundred dollars' worth of used clothes.

Outside the store, I asked her how much her parents had sent.

"A thousand bucks. Why?"

I shrugged, and we walked on, passing a used book and record store. I stared a little too long at the display window.

"You want to go in?"

"No, I'm OK."

She dragged me by the sleeve.

"We're going in!"

We emerged an hour later with a dozen LPs, two books on bird watching and a huge laminated *Flashdance* poster of Jennifer Beals' shower scene. "My favourite movie!" squealed Saké. I wasn't surprised.

We were loaded up like mules, but Saké insisted on going to the bakery opposite the store. She ordered ten plain and ten chocolate croissants; two loaves of bread, one with sunflower seeds, the other with olives; a cheesecake; and a lemon pie. We walked home. My arms were aching from carrying so much stuff and my ribcage felt a little sore. I lay down on the couch, while Saké sat on the floor and tried on her wigs. I told her then about the surgery, and about the cramps.

"Are you having one now?"

"Yes. Not quite as bad as usual, though."

I paused.

"I've never told anyone before. About the cramps."

"Why? You don't want your parents to know?"

"I'd rather they didn't. They'd get worried and make me go see more specialists. I've had enough. I never asked for anything, and I know they mean well, but playing the lab rat pisses me off... And for what? I don't feel any better than before. I never even felt that bad, really... they were the ones who worried. I suppose they were right. I am a little rough around the edges, but I'm OK with the way I am. I don't want to change just to make them happy."

"I'm sorry. For earlier. I didn't know."

"Sorry for what?"

"For having you try on all those clothes."

"Oh that... Don't worry: it's all good."

We snacked on the croissants and watched TV while waiting for my parents. The Jupiter documentary was on again. It fascinated me to think that you could pick up signals from Jupiter with nothing more than a shortwave radio and a dipole antenna. They sounded like waves breaking on a beach. I promised myself I'd try it soon. When the documentary was over, I turned off the TV.

"How much do you have left?"

Saké went through her pockets and threw a wad of cash over the floor. I helped her count.

"Two hundred and sixty five. Not too shabby."

"And what are your plans now?"

"I'm trying to save up to move to San Francisco for a while."

She sprang up, as if she'd just had a eureka moment.

"You should come with me!"

"What would we do in San Francisco?"

"I don't know. I asked a couple of people at work if they could recommend me to a hair studio over there. They have connections. Nothing's settled, but even if the studio thing falls through, I'm going all the same. I'll sift through the classifieds. Join a band and play the tambourine. And you could become a journalist and write about the underground music scene or whatever. We'll spend whole afternoons doing fuck all. Raid second-hand stores in Haight-Ashbury. I'll paint massive frescoes and we'll be rich. You'll be my agent and negotiate with galleries for me. We'll eat late at night and sleep all day. Rob banks and go to the movies in the morning. We'll buy a car and dump it in the ocean. Climb hills and throw confetti to the wind. I'll learn Spanish, you'll learn Russian, and we'll sing folk songs in the cable cars. We'll feed the seagulls on Alcatraz and swim across the bay. I'll enroll at Berkeley and get kicked out because I can't pay my tuition. And you'll become a ballet dancer."

"OK," I said. "OK, we'll go. How much money did you save?"

My sudden enthusiasm caught her off guard.

"Er… I'm not sure. Not enough yet, a thousand, maybe two?"

"Perfect. That'll give me time to put some aside as well. And what about school?"

"I'm almost done. I graduate at the end of the semester. You?"

"I've a ways to go, but that doesn't matter. Let's wait a few months, OK?"

"Sure, a couple more months."

We got up at the same time and shook hands to make it official.

After my shift, I went to the park, where Chokichi was waiting for me.

"Hey! How's it going?"

"Meh. My folks kicked me out of the house."

Chokichi told me everything: his parents had found out their son was selling cocaine and other drugs. They'd thrown him out, yelling that he was a disgrace to the family and they didn't want to hear from him until he'd gotten his act together.

"So I was wondering… Could I crash at yours for a while?"

"I'd be glad to take you in. Not too sure about my parents, though. Saké just moved in. I'll have to ask them first."

He handed me a cigarette. We smoked in silence. The old swings creaked in the wind. The street was empty, the park was deserted, night had fallen and the sky was starless, as usual. I wondered if the sky was just as bare in San Francisco, if you could actually see Jupiter, and not just hear its waves on the radio.

I broke the news to Chokichi straight off: "I'm moving to San Francisco with Saké."

"What?"

"Not now, in a few months. I don't know for how long. Until then, I'll be working a few more shifts at the graveyard to save enough cash to pay the rent when we're over there, while we look for a job, or something else to do."

"Wait, not so fast. Rewind."

"Rewind what?"

"You, moving to San Fran... Where did that come from?"

"I don't know. Saké mentioned it today, and er... I just want to try and do something with my life, you know? Something a bit wild. Don't you ever wish you could get lost, just to be able to find yourself again? I don't want a different life, just a little break, a new reason to wake up in the morning."

"You're never up before noon, Holly."

"Very funny."

"OK, sure, I get it."

"Well, I'm dying to go with her now, so it'd be stupid not to jump at the chance."

We talked it over a while longer, until I felt like going home to lie on the balcony and listen to music, and clear my mind. But Chokichi pointed to his bag, which reminded me he had nowhere to go. I borrowed his phone.

Saké answered.

"Hello?"

"It's me."

"Holly, hi!"

"Are my parents in bed yet?"

"No, they're baking muffins."

"Really?"

"What do *you* think? It's one o'clock in the morning, Holly. Of course they're in bed. Why?"

"Chokichi got kicked out of his parents' house. I wanted to ask them if he could stay with us until he finds something better."

"OK, he can take the couch."

"Still, I'll have to ask Mom and Dad tomorrow..."

"Hey, wait a second!"

"What?"

"Rajani and Arnaud—there's a guest room at their place. Call you back in ten."

She hung up without asking where I was calling from. Since there wasn't much chance of her knowing Chokichi's number, we walked over to the apartment. Saké waved at us from the balcony.

"Wait up! I'm on my way!"

She came to meet us on the sidewalk a good ten minutes later.

"What the hell were you doing up there?"

"I forgot to turn off the TV and got distracted by this movie. Seemed too good to miss."

"So did you talk to Rajani?"

"Yeah, and they're cool with it. We can go there right now. They had friends over, but they just left."

We walked to Rajani's. Arnaud opened the door holding a tray full of olives and crackers.

"Come on in and eat! There's an insane amount of food left!"

He shooed the three of us into the kitchen. Rajani was almost done washing the dishes. The table was covered with food: appetizers (tapenade, yet more olives, stuffed artichoke hearts, trays of mussels with mayo, salted preserves, rabbit terrine), mutton cassoulet, sea bream in tomato sauce, crab bisque, anchovy pie and of course a choice of desserts: rice pudding, strawberry meringue pie and almond tuiles with apricot sauce. There were plenty of bottles of wine, most of them empty, some barely touched. While Arnaud was describing the *menu du jour*, Rajani gave a round of hugs and we all sat down at the table.

"How many people did you have over?" I asked.

"There were four of us. Two friends, Rajani and me."

Rajani quickly explained the evening's theme: Provence, where Arnaud was from. He'd gotten carried away and cooked for two days straight; now they had leftovers for a week. Saké grabbed a slice of strawberry pie and I served myself a generous portion of sea bream. Chokichi was coaxed into eating something, and he finally opted for a bowl of soup and a few mussels. Arnaud munched on olives as he watched us eat.

"I didn't even know you were French," said Saké between bites. "You have no accent."

"I've been here a long time. I was five when my family left Toulon. My grandmother still lives there. I go and visit her every other year, more or less. She taught me how to cook."

We ate in silence until Chokichi put his cards on the table.

"So... Saké said you'd let me rent a room for a while."

They discussed the rent and how long he'd be staying while I stuffed myself with sea bream and almond tuiles. I drank a few glasses of wine and suddenly felt exhausted. A cramp tore through my chest. Saké noticed. She stood and made up an excuse to leave, saying she had something to do early the next day. I followed her to the front door. We all kissed each other goodbye like close friends, and I left Chokichi with Rajani and Arnaud. Saké and I caught a bus home. It was 4 a.m. Night was already fading into day; it looked like this would be yet another sunny, intensely hot day. I felt worn out. I looked out the window all through the five-minute ride home. I dragged my feet upstairs and Saké was kind enough not to comment. We wished each other goodnight and I locked myself in my room without even going to the bathroom to brush my teeth. I put a Joni Mitchell album, *For the Roses*, on the old record player and set the needle down on the first groove of *You Turn Me On I'm a Radio*. I fell asleep midway through the next song, *Blonde in the Bleachers*. I hadn't gone to sleep so fast in a very long time.

Hollywood

UNDERGROUND POEM #12

my body shrouded in mist
and I will dwell in a period film
for here I stand, in black and white, on a road never taken

After the sandman

THEY REMAIN STANDING FOR SOME TIME before the hole in the window, watching the meteor shower. They say nothing. They both believe that, at this rate, the sky will eventually burn out. Then Hollywood shouts:

"It's cold in here!"

"But it isn't snowing. It's stopped."

Xavier

I FELT LIKE DANCING. And that seemed both beautiful and silly. I'd always looked down on people whose moods vary with the weather. This time, though, I couldn't resist. The sun was shining and I felt like dancing.

Antony agreed to come with me to the hospital, partly because he didn't believe my story and partly because we had nothing to do all day. Pullman had booked us plane tickets in business class, but we'd have to wait until the following night because the sky was too crowded: it seemed everyone wanted to go back to America at the same time, and now that air traffic had resumed all flights were bursting at the seams.

We stopped at the hotel to change into more comfortable clothes, then called a cab. Barely five minutes later, we pulled up at the hospital. I bought a bouquet from the florist on the first floor, and we headed to Gia's room.

It was empty. I flagged down a nurse in the hallway, who explained that Gia had left that morning; these days new mothers aren't kept long at the hospital if their babies are healthy. I asked if Gia had left a phone number where I could reach her. *Estos datos son confidenciales,* I was told with a sigh of exasperation, first in Spanish, then in English and finally in French. The nurse escorted Antony and me to the hospital's main entrance and planted herself at the door, waiting to make sure we left.

"Bitch!" I shouted, sitting down on the sidewalk. "She could have at least given me her phone number... I wasn't looking for her address or social insurance number."

"Well, if this was a soap opera or a TV drama, I would sneak in the back and steal her address and phone number from the nurse's desk," Antony observed. "*Veux-tu que j'essaie?*"

"No, that's OK." I sighed.

Antony offered me a cigarette and put his arm around my shoulders. I smoked in silence, and then we got up. I threw the flowers in the nearest trash can. We walked back to the hotel, where we parted ways; Antony felt like going out, so we said goodnight.

I climbed onto the bed with the Telepizza menu I'd found on the nightstand and ordered two pizzas, fries, a few sandwiches, two bottles of Coke and a chocolate tart. I'd have enough to survive until the next day.

I asked reception to send up the food as soon as it came; in the meantime, I felt like grabbing a short workout in the hotel gym and trying the Turkish baths they'd told us about when we checked in.

I jumped on a stationary bike for a few minutes, but quickly tired of it. The Turkish bath reeked of eucalyptus, giving me a wave of nausea. I walked past the pool and had a sudden urge to swim, but I hadn't brought my bathing suit and had no desire to go back to my room to get it. I made sure there was nobody changing in the locker room—not the men's, not the women's—and stripped down; I plunged into the water completely naked. And of course, after only three laps, a family of four walked in. I swam even faster: if I kept moving, they might not notice I was naked as a jaybird. The mother sat down on a chair with her book and the father splashed around with his two young children. I waited until no one was looking before hopping out of the water and making a beeline for the locker room. I dried off and went back down to my room, towel around my waist, my clothes rolled up into a ball.

A mountain of food was waiting for me on the desk. I put on some underwear, opened a box of pizza and ordered a movie: *Breakfast at Tiffany's*. I emptied a small bottle of Cuban rum into a tall glass, then filled it to the brim with Coke. I drank at least ten of these while I watched the movie and finished off the pizza. I was pissed off with life again, but I can't resist Audrey Hepburn so I couldn't help feeling a little sentimental.

Those big brown eyes, her hats and sunglasses, her funny accent, those ridiculously posh gloves, the jewellery and Givenchy dresses, her eyelashes and her smile, the long cigarette holder—I'm mesmerized every time. I even managed to forgive how much tamer the movie is compared to the Capote novel, not to mention Mickey Rooney's godawful performance, and I sang along to *Moon River*, my mouth full of cheese and tomato sauce. I may not be the society doll that Holly Golightly is, half birdbrain, half call girl, but in a fit of narcissism I found myself identifying with her character, enough to catch myself dreaming of love stories of my own while the credits rolled. Any story would do. Anything but my own.

::

"What are you taking to sleep?" Antony asked.

"Same as you."

He slipped two pills into my hand. I ordered a scotch on ice from the flight attendant. I was asleep twenty minutes later.

We landed in Toronto just in time: the snow had started up again. The second area of low pressure Paloma had mentioned on France 2 had moved from the Great Lakes up to the Golden Horseshoe.

Since Antony lives in Cabbagetown and I live in West Queen West, we shared a taxi back; two hours later it dropped me off in front of my apartment building before continuing on with Antony. I went up and threw my suitcases onto the living room floor. I looked out at the snow falling in the park across the street. Then I closed the curtains and lay down on the bed without bothering to take off my coat or shoes. It's a habit of mine, and whenever I'm in the mood for a little tragedy I just switch off like that—somehow it seems to suit my lousy existence.

I woke up in the middle of the night, at 3:37 a.m. I boiled water and made myself an enormous mug of mandarin orange green tea. I turned on a few lamps here and there and chose a DVD at random from my collection: *Bonnie and Clyde* starring Warren Beatty and Faye Dunaway. I rummaged around in the fridge, but I'd been gone so long everything had either grown mould or dried up. I threw out salmon, a few tomatoes, the leftover cottage cheese, a couple of lemons, a batch of vegetable broth, a bunch of celery stalks, chicken and a carton of milk. I took a few cans and a box of pasta from the pantry and whipped up macaroni with tomato and yellow beans, which I sprinkled with Parmesan and fresh-ground black pepper. I ate straight from the pot to save on clean-up, sitting on the floor in front of the TV. When it became clear that Bonnie and Clyde were done for, I opened my suitcase and started emptying its contents onto the floor. I made piles: clean clothes, dirty clothes, toiletries, passport and other ID, receipts to keep, ones to throw away, etc. Then, at the very bottom, I found a little pouch of potpourri that I didn't remember packing.

Actually, I was sure I hadn't put it there myself because I hate potpourri; the smell gives me such a headache it takes ages to go away. I got up to throw it in the trash. I untied the ribbon that held the net together and poured the contents over the food I'd just thrown away. A piece of white paper fell out, together with a cinnamon stick and a glazed apple peel. I picked it out of the garbage and stared. A phone number had been scribbled on it: 514.103.3390. I was sure it was Gia.

There was no answer, so I left a message. I gave her both my home and my cell numbers and decided not to leave the house until she called. If she'd given me her Montreal number it must mean she'd be back soon.

Since I still hadn't heard from her the next day, I did some research on the Internet and read that you usually had to wait about three weeks before flying with a newborn. Unless Gia had taken a boat back to America—unlikely—I'd have to wait a bit longer for her to return my call. So I left a new message explaining what I'd just found out and offering to visit her in Montreal when she arrived. I gave her my email address before hanging up.

I was supposed to meet Pullman the Monday after I got back, which was the next day. I was sick of eating macaroni and yellow beans, so I walked to the grocery store. It normally takes fifteen minutes, but it took me thirty-five with all the snow and wind. A streetcar had gotten stuck at the corner of King and Strachan, and a team of TTC employees was trying to clear the track.

The snow was piling up almost as quickly as they were ploughing it away.

I took a cab back since I'd just bought nearly two hundred dollars' worth of groceries, enough food to last until Gia decided to call me back. Antony had left a message while I was out, asking if I was up for drinks at the Park Hyatt after the meeting. I politely declined: I'd rather stay home. I'm expecting an important call, but you can come over if you want.

::

I asked Pullman for two months off and was shocked when he agreed. *You made two big sales, you deserve it.* I was all ready to negotiate, to accept unpaid leave for the last-minute vacation, but I didn't bat an eyelash when he offered me pay at fifty percent. He handed me four big binders to study while I was gone, new products the company was adding to its catalogue. Antony, meanwhile, was given a hefty bonus provided he left again soon. Pullman wanted him to represent the company at a conference in Aruba, which was right up his alley.

We took the 501 Queen streetcar back to my place, but decided to get off a block early. Antony wanted to grab pierogies from Czehoski's.

"They stuff 'em with sweet potato and smoked gouda, man. They're the best I've ever had!"

We sat at the bar and I ordered a beer and a plate of oysters. We ate, drank our fill and then walked back to my place.

"Nothing much gets me going other than food, booze and DVDs," I sighed, collapsing onto the couch. "Sometimes I wish I could be more like you."

"What do you mean, be more like me?"

"I don't know... stop questioning everything and just live my life like everyone else."

"So you think I'm just a happy-go-lucky moron?"

"No, you know that's not what I mean. But you're happy with what you have and what you do. And I can't be like that."

"Man, I hope these two months off will do you good, 'cause now you're kind of a bummer to talk to. *T'es peut-être fatigué, non?*"

"Yeah, that must be it..."

I wanted to change the subject instead of embarking on a conversation neither of us wanted to have. Antony picked out Hitchcock's *Strangers on a Train* from my collection, and we watched it and drank mulled wine. He dozed off before the end and I let him sleep on the couch. I went to lie down in my bed, but couldn't sleep. I didn't want to take sleeping pills, so I turned on the TV on my dresser and watched a documentary about Jupiter until I fell asleep from exhaustion.

Xavier

When he told me he was moving to San Francisco it seemed like he was worried I'd be disappointed or angry. I don't think it will change anything about our nighttime encounters, I replied. And that gave me an idea: I'm going to make a change, too. I'll sell my apartment and move to Montreal.

Be a little more proactive—like the people in the movies, or even in real life, who ditch everything for someone they've just met. Even if most of the time it doesn't end well.

He said it's been summer for almost a year in Montreal. I told him it's been snowing out west for weeks. Then we both brought up the same stories, the same news reports, the ones we knew about despite our mutual lack of interest in the world around us.

By day, I skate circles. In every sense.

Hollywood

EVER SINCE I DECIDED TO LEAVE, everything's been getting on my nerves. I suppose it's normal. Still, I really want to get the hell out of here as soon as I can. I asked for a bunch of extra shifts at the graveyard so that I can save up more quickly. And I dropped out of school. I won't be graduating at the end of the semester anyway, so there's no point in studying, handing in projects or going to class if I can rake the grounds and plant beans at the graveyard, read astronomy books while listening to music until dawn and then sleep until noon and rake the grounds and plant beans at the graveyard, read astronomy books and so on.

"Did you know that more than sixty forest fires are burning right now in Quebec? In February!"
I took a bite of bread.

"No wonder, with that heat. What puzzles me, though, is that no one is even surprised anymore. It's thirty degrees out! On February 27!"

"Do you think it can last much longer?" asked Saké.

"How should I know? I don't have a clue."

Saké took one last sip of orange juice. She had the morning off. She'd gotten up shortly before me, around noon, and made breakfast for the both of us.

"It won't be as hot in San Francisco," she said.

I nodded, mumbling with my mouth full. Sure, it probably won't be as hot over there. And there will be fog.

Saké picked up a pile of papers lying on the counter.

"I found this in your room last night. I was looking for a book, or a magazine, or whatever, and this is what I came across."

She tossed the papers on the table.

"I didn't know you wrote poetry! That's just perfect!"

I was too intrigued by her comment to even think about bristling at the violation of my privacy.

"It's perfect? What do you mean it's perfect?"

"For San Francisco..."

"Huh?"

"There's a bunch of poets over there. You could make a living out of it, publishing your poems."

"Nobody writes poetry to earn a living."

"Why then?"

"Er... I don't know. Because some things can't be said any other way."

She looked confused, but it seemed pretty straightforward to me.

"Anyway, I don't want to publish those poems. Plus I wrote them in French: nobody will want to read them."

I got up and put my plate in the sink.

"Are you going to wash the dishes?" I asked.

"No way! I made breakfast! *You* clean up!"

I put on a record in my room and cranked the volume to the max. I left the door open to hear the music better from the kitchen. Saké had decided to work out in the living room; we'd picked the album together. Something that would help her go all out jazzercising, and allow my thoughts to wander while I washed the dishes. I suggested Joni Mitchell; Saké wanted something with a stronger beat, better suited for a workout: Wild Cherry it was. *Play That Funky Music.*

As I was scrubbing a pan Saké had used for goodness knows what, my heart suddenly felt like it had just beaten. I knew that was impossible since I don't have a heart anymore, but that's what it felt like: a strange pulse in my chest, nothing like the cramps I get from time to time. I was so startled I lost my balance and had to cling to the counter so that I wouldn't fall. I breathed in deeply and checked my pulse or whatever; everything seemed normal. Maybe the little machine they'd put inside of me had started up for a moment, making up for a drop in blood pressure or something? I waited for a few minutes, first for the song to end, then to make sure that I wasn't about to die. Only then did I go on scrubbing the pan. Too late: I'd lost touch with reality. I was aware that I was washing the dishes, that Saké was dancing in the living room and that *Don't Go Near the Water* was belting out through the speakers in my bedroom. But none of it made sense. It was as if nothing, in itself, truly existed: the objects around me, the things I was still doing, the music... It all looked and felt a certain way because of how my brain *perceived* it. If I ceased to exist, if I stopped breathing, what would become of it all?

I tried to shake off the thought. It made me dizzy. I sat down on the floor, with my back against the cupboards, and closed my eyes.

"Er... What are you doing on the floor?"

I opened my eyes. Saké was standing at my feet, sweating, panting. I lifted myself up on my elbows and smiled.

"Nothing."

Then I got up and went back to scrubbing the pan.

"Would you *please* tell me what you burnt here?" I asked, waving the pan.

"I wanted to make eggs Benedict. First I messed up the eggs, then I forgot about the hollandaise on the stove while I was trying to fry the ham. I dumped it all."

Hollywood

UNDERGROUND POEM #13

I cannot see
the sea from my bed

back to being a ghost

After the sandman

THIS TIME THEY MEET IN XAVIER'S APARTMENT. It's the first time they've seen each other somewhere other than a hotel room. They're both a little uncomfortable, like lovers sharing a piece of everyday life for the first time. They decide to take a walk. That's also a first. They rarely move. They usually sit and talk for a while before disappearing.

It was snowing when Xavier fell asleep, but in his dream there isn't a cloud in the sky. The city is dark; the lights have all gone out. They walk with their faces turned to the sky, which is still streaked with light. They don't want to miss such a beautiful display. The stars fall like rain.

"Do you think it's all real?"

"The shooting stars?"

"That too. But I mean our dreams. Are they dreams, or something else?"

Xavier doesn't reply right away. They stop in front of a bus shelter. Hollywood sits down before going on.

"Back home, it's summer. You'll say that's impossible in February. But it's summer. In February. Here it's cold, there's snow... so it should be a dream. Usually my dreams are much more jumbled up and I can barely remember what they were about. But when I wake up in a few minutes, I'll remember everything we did and everything we said."

"I know..."

Xavier's phone rings. They both jump.

"It's my boss; I have to take it."

Hollywood gets up and wanders off. The night is fading; the sky slowly turns from black to blue. The stars are disappearing. The streaks of light are dissolving, becoming less and less frequent. And yet there is still no light in the surrounding buildings. The power must be out.

Xavier hangs up and motions Hollywood back.

"I've got to go to New York the day after tomorrow. It's an emergency: a company rep was in a pretty serious car accident. I'm the only one who can replace him."

Xavier

I WOKE UP A LITTLE BEFORE NOON and immediately checked my phone to make sure that it was just a dream, that Pullman hadn't called me in the middle of the night, that I wouldn't have to pack up and leave for New York that afternoon. There was a message: an Amtrak train leaving the next morning from Union Station at 8:30, arriving that night in New York Penn Station at 9:35. Pullman wrote: "I couldn't find a ride for this afternoon so you're leaving tomorrow morning. I'll have someone pick you up at Penn Station to bring you to the hotel. I sent you the literature about the drug by messenger this morning. You should get it soon. Sorry this is not air travel; I figured the train would be more reliable given the weather." I hadn't been dreaming. Well actually yes, I had been. I hopped into the shower and turned the cold water up, trying to get my head around it all. The doorbell rang. I turned off the water, wrapped a towel around my waist and went to answer.

"Special delivery for Mr. Xavier Adam," a man in a red and yellow uniform announced.

I signed the electronic pad he held out to me. He turned and left, leaving me with a large binder: the literature on the drug I was to present in New York. I sat down at the kitchen table to flip through it: a gastrointestinal motility stimulant to treat constipation. Thrilling.

I called Gia again before getting dressed. Still no answer, but the voicemail didn't click on. Had she cancelled it without listening to my messages? I dialled again to make sure it wasn't the wrong number. No answer, even after thirty rings. I gave up and went to put on some clothes.

I walked to a nearby café and sat down with a goji berry green tea. I opened the binder and read a few pages, but the material was dull and I was much more interested in what was going on outside. I watched passersby battle their way through the snow. I was surprised that the downtown offices and stores were still open in this weather. I was bored as hell so I threw the binder into my bag, asked for a to-go cup for the tea and walked back home.

I packed a few pairs of shoes, clothes, toiletries and the binder. I'd have more than enough time to look it over on the train or at the hotel before the pitch. Antony called just as I was closing my suitcase.

"*T'es libre?*" he asked.

"Yup. Nothing planned until tomorrow morning."

"OK. Meet me at the Pegasus on Church Street."

He hung up. I threw on a coat and called a cab. I didn't feel like walking the hour or so it would take to get there.

I waited downstairs in the lobby for over twenty minutes before the car showed up. I ducked into the backseat and gave the driver the directions.

Antony was already two drinks deep when I arrived.

"So. You're off to New York City tomorrow?"

I nodded.

"I'm not especially pleased, but Pullman didn't give me a choice."

"*Oui, il m'a dit.* But you'll be happy when you get your bonus."

A pool table opened up, so we got up and started a game.

"When do you leave?" I asked.

"Tonight at eight, with a connection in Charlotte. Landing tomorrow morning in hot, sunny Aruba! No more snow for me!"

We played a few rounds, had a few drinks, talked a bit. I was jealous that Antony got to escape this never-ending blizzard. Usually the snow didn't bother me; it hadn't bothered me too much in London or Bilbao. But the short let-up just before I'd come back to Toronto had poisoned my thoughts, so to speak, and I couldn't stop thinking about white sand beaches and crystal blue water. I hoped March would bring some sun and that it would finally stop snowing.

Around 5 p.m. Antony took a taxi to the airport. I was tired and hungry. I left the bar and walked across the street to Baskin Robbins, where I bought a fudge crunch cake to take home. I walked over to the university campus and went into the first building that seemed inviting. I sat down on a bench and ate nearly half of the cake. I gave the rest to a passing student, who probably threw it in the nearest garbage can. I didn't give a shit. I left. It was colder now; the wind had picked up. I pulled the collar of my coat up over my ears and walked to the subway. I collapsed onto one of the seats and fell asleep even before the train reached the next station.

I woke up at the end of the line, far from home. It was almost 8 p.m. I went up to street level and walked down Yonge for a few minutes, then went into a Korean restaurant. I ordered sushi and a soup. I picked at the food, but wasn't really hungry. I called a cab. Again.

Two hours later I was home. I turned on the TV, lay down on the couch and fell asleep.

::

The train left on schedule, despite the snow, the wind and the blizzard. Though it was warm in the cars, I kept both my coat and scarf on; they came round with a glass of port on the house, *courtesy of Amtrak, to thank you all for your business.* I sank back into the seat and connected to the Wi-Fi network on my cellphone. I found videos of the Mariinsky Ballet dancing *The Nutcracker*. The windows were covered in frost so it was impossible to see the landscape racing by, but I felt good, like it was Christmas again. It was like a scene from an indie flick, the kind that takes place in New York (where else?) just a few days before Christmas. All I needed was the dysfunctional family and I would have myself a near-perfect holiday feature film. I watched the *Waltz of the Flowers* with my mind completely blank. Life was good.

A driver was waiting for me at Penn Station holding a large white card with my name printed in big black letters. Until that moment nothing like that had ever happened to me; I thought that kind of thing was only for characters in romantic comedies. My mundane life was suddenly looking more and more like a scene from a movie. The driver took me to the Hilton Garden Inn Chelsea, about a two-minute trip. I checked in at the reception desk and was given a key as well as information on the comforts my stay included. I went right up to the room; it was late, and I was tired. I'd barely had time to drop my bags on the bed when the phone rang. I answered, thinking it was the front desk calling because I'd left something on the counter.

"Xavier?"

"Yes. That's me."

"Xavier? It's me."

I recognized the accent immediately.

"Gia?"

"Xavier, I don't have much time. I'm in rehearsal. Do you have something to write with?"

"Yeah, sure. But hang on, wait—how do you know I'm here? I just got in..."

"Can you meet me tomorrow night? I'll be at the Soho Repertory Theatre, 46 Walker Street, between Church and Broadway, south of Canal. Ask the concierge how to get there. The dress rehearsal ends at 9:30. You can come for around 10:15, that will give me enough time to change and get cleaned up."

She hung up. I listened to the ring tone for a few seconds before resigning myself to do the same. I'd jotted down the information she'd given me on a piece of paper stamped with the hotel letterhead. I threw myself onto the bed, staring at the words I'd scribbled.

Xavier

I find the silence of hotel rooms unnerving, but turning on the TV helps relieve the stress of not being at home. And at home it's the same thing. I only find solace in the TV droning on and on. A movie I don't even watch. A silly program that's on while I'm trying to go about my life. To help me forget that there's no great misfortune to blame, nothing to explain my beautifully blasé attitude. An expression I heard in a dream, I think, which seems accurate, fitting and absolutely true.

I'm no one and nothing—just beautifully blasé. And I don't belong anywhere.

If words sometimes fail to express my discomfort, I think an image might do it justice. A simple pencil drawing, in shades of grey. A #2 pencil like the ones we were told to buy in elementary school. With a bit of practice, I might be able to come up with a picture that would say it all: in the background, brick buildings with their windows illuminated. The deserted street lit by a series of street lamps casting a round glow on the sidewalk, like the spotlights used on stage to illuminate a particular actor. And then me, seen from the back; I'd be standing under the only lamp that didn't work, in the shadows.

But I'm hopeless with perspective.

Hollywood

I WOKE UP ONE MORNING, and she was gone. I mean: all her things had disappeared, her room was tidy, her bed had been made. She was gone. I looked inside the fridge, where she usually leaves a note if she needs to tell me something: nothing but a sad-looking leek. I thought she'd left without me because she was done waiting, period.

I fished a big suitcase out of my parents' closet. I threw in all my clothes, a toothbrush, a tube of toothpaste, a towel, a few pencils, a large notebook, the poems I'd written, Joni Mitchell's biography (which I still hadn't finished), a Leonard Cohen novel, my iPod and earbuds, a pack of cigarettes and a bottle of Gardenal. I got dressed and left the house. Twenty-eight degrees on the first of March. Birds were chirping in the yellow wheat. Chickadees and house sparrows.

I walked over to Chokichi's new digs at Rajani and Arnaud's. On the way, I realized I'd forgotten to leave my parents a note. I'd call them once I got there, I told myself, but only if it was absolutely necessary. There was no need to worry about my job: my 'clients' were all dead and buried; they wouldn't miss me too much. And the beans would go on growing without me, unless the graveyard hired someone who preferred neat lawns to pulses.

I knocked a few times before Chokichi came to the door: stripped to the waist, his hair dishevelled, still half asleep.

"Did I wake you?"

He let me in without saying a word. I followed him into the kitchen. There was some coffee left in the percolator. He poured himself a cup and asked if I wanted one.

"No thanks."

He sunk into a chair.

"I spent the night writing an essay for a class I'm taking. I handed it in this morning around eight. So I went to bed... two hours ago," he said, turning to look at the clock behind him.

"I came to say... goodbye to you, my trusted friend."

"Just like in the song!"

He giggled.

"Yeah, like the song! 'We had joy, we had fun, we had seasons in the sun...'"

"But seriously, you came to say *goodbye*? Are you going somewhere?"

I pointed to my suitcase.

"San Francisco."

"Right *now*?"

"Well... I think so. I'm not sure anymore."

"Not sure about *what*? I'm still half asleep here. You're gonna have to spell it out for me."

"Yeah, sorry."

I told him Saké had left during the night, and I'd decided to skip town too.

"But why are you saying you're not sure? Are you going or not?"

"I am. When I realized Saké had already split, I knew I had to leave too, as soon as possible. If I keep waiting, I'll never do it. But I'm not sure I should be going to San Francisco anymore."

"Why not?"

"Because. If Saké left me behind, maybe she wanted to go alone."

"Makes sense. If not, she would've waited for you, or left you a note."

He jumped up.

"I'll be right back."

He ran over to his bedroom. I got up and paced the kitchen.

"Rajani and Arnaud aren't here?" I shouted.

"Nope. Arnaud's at work and Rajani has a class," Chokichi shouted back.

I opened the fridge and made a sandwich with what I could find. I'd forgotten to have breakfast. I made one for Chokichi too. He came back a few minutes later, dressed and shaved with his hair brushed and a sports bag over his shoulder. He took the sandwich I held out, and smiled at me.

"Come on, we're leaving."

He pushed me out the door. I waited until we were outside to ask where we were off to.

"I don't know. We'll figure it out when we get to the bus station."

Hollywood

UNDERGROUND POEM #18

the wind is warm
—as always—
when we leave the bus at last

I am an ominous dream

After the sandman

THEY ARE TORN FROM THE PLACES we find them: one, the dormitory of a Chicago hostel; the other, the room of a New York hotel.

"I've got a feeling something's brewing. Don't you?"

"Brewing? Maybe not," says Xavier. "But something's definitely happening right now."

They are quiet for a few minutes.

"Where are we?"

"I have no idea."

Part two

Montauk

"I DIDN'T SEE ANYONE ON THE BEACH or on the street. No one in the grocery store either. All the stores and restaurants are closed. We're in Montauk; I saw it on a street sign."

"Montauk? Montauk in the Hamptons?" asks Xavier.

"That's the one."

"How'd we get here?"

"I have no idea."

Hollywood drops the supplies on the table: garlic, tomatoes, spaghetti, cheese, a bottle of red wine, a loaf of bread, chocolate. The essentials.

"The grocery store wasn't locked. I took what we needed for tonight. I'll go back tomorrow, maybe someone will be there so I can explain and pay. It's not that cold, it was a nice walk. The village is only thirty minutes away on foot."

"I couldn't get the scooter to start. Maybe we can buy gas tomorrow and fill it up."

"You think that's the problem?"

"Maybe. I don't know the first thing about mechanics."

Xavier rummages through the kitchen drawers, comes up with a corkscrew and opens the bottle of wine. Hollywood takes two big glasses from the cabinet and Xavier fills them up. He takes a sip before telling Hollywood what he did while he was gone.

"I explored the place: it's a beach house that's closed for the winter. The gas is on, and I found some wood in the shed out back to light a fire. It was pretty easy to turn on the power: the electrical box is under the porch, you just have to use the big red lever. The closets are full of clothes, but only summer clothes. I found polos and pants to wear while we do laundry. There are two bathrooms, one in each bedroom. The piano in the living room is tuned. Or at least it doesn't sound too bad to my inexperienced ear. No phone or TV."

"So we won't freeze to death. Or starve, if we figure out how to make some money."

"That's the best part: I found *this* in the main bedroom."

Xavier slaps a large envelope onto the kitchen island.

"Wow! Did you count it?"

Hollywood thumbs through the banknotes in his hands.

"Yeah. Close to ten thousand."

"Enough to get the hell out of here!" Hollywood announces.

"That's what I was thinking, too."

"Want to eat outside tonight? We could light a few candles, if we find some. I've never eaten in front of the ocean."

"I bet I can scrounge up a few candles. We can grab the little table from the shed. I'll do it. You want to take care of dinner?"

"Sure. I got stuff to make pasta with tomato sauce. I don't have a lot of imagination in the kitchen. There are a few restaurants in town. If they're open next time, we could eat out in the square or in one of the places on the main street. Especially if you manage to get the scooter going."

Xavier puts on a coat and boots.

"I should go out before it gets too dark."

::

It's pretty normal for March, if it really is March. Around five degrees Celsius. Still a little snow on the ground. The sand and rocks are bare, licked clean by the sea. Although snow covers the dunes, tall grass pokes up through the white carpet. The stars blink on and off, like tiny lights. Xavier and Hollywood don't speak much; they don't know what to make of it all yet.

"We could head to the train station tomorrow. I'd like to get back to New York," says Xavier. "I have a feeling I missed an important meeting."

The sun has been down for a few hours. The cold wind coming off the sea has made the temperature drop. The candle flame flickers dangerously. Xavier and Hollywood are shivering in their coats. The waves wash up and die on the beach; otherwise, there isn't a sound. In the distance, they can barely make out the glow of the lighthouse on Montauk Point.

"I'm going in before I freeze to death," Xavier says. "I'm sick of winter."

He gets up. Hollywood follows, picking up their plates.

"I'll take care of the dishes. Could you make a fire?"

They walk into the house. Hollywood washes their plates while Xavier lights a fire. The room warms instantly.

"Can you play the piano?" he asks Hollywood as he flops onto the sofa.

"No. I've tried, but it never works. My hands never seem to be on the same page."

He sits at the piano and picks out a nursery rhyme, stumbling as he plays.

"See? I'm terrible."

He lowers the cover over the keyboard and leans on it.

"What about you? Do you know how to play?"

"No," says Xavier, then adds, "It's a shame... such a lovely piano, and it's no good to us."

"Find any books or CDs?" Hollywood asks.

"There's a huge bookcase in the den. And the turntable's in the corner."

"Excellent! I brought something to read, but apparently my bag doesn't follow me into my dreams..."

"Do you still think we're dreaming?"

"I have no idea. What about you?"

"I try not to think about it."

Hollywood gets up and goes into the next room to peruse the bookshelves.

"Do you like classical music?" he asks Xavier, who hasn't moved.

"Not really."

"Then you'll need to get used to it: that's all there is."

"You can put on whatever you want, I don't mind. I'll head to bed, if that's OK. I'm sleepy."

"That's weird, though," Hollywood thinks aloud. "If we were in a dream, we wouldn't need to sleep..."

"But since I'm tired... maybe we really are here, after all. What I don't understand is how and why we ended up in Montauk."

Hollywood puts a recording of Pergolesi's *Stabat Mater* on the turntable, then comes back into the living room. He lies down on the sofa.

"I'm going to sleep here. I don't really know the house well enough yet, and the small bedroom gives me the creeps."

"You can take the big one if you want," Xavier offers.

"No, that's OK. You take it. The sofa seems comfortable. I'll grab a pillow and a blanket later, when I'm ready to go to sleep."

"OK. Goodnight."

"Goodnight."

A cramp rips through his chest. *The machine,* he thinks. *Either it turned on, or it's acting up.* The *Stabat Mater* is over. The disc is still spinning, but the needle is hanging in the air. Hollywood gets up and shuts off the turntable. He turns out the lights and lies back down on the sofa. The silence weighs on his chest. He breathlessly hums a Leonard Cohen tune, quietly, as if to soothe himself. Then he falls asleep.

When Xavier comes out of his room a few hours later, eyes red from lack of sleep, troubled by insomnia, Hollywood is gone.

Hollywood

"SORRY, SWEETIE: the A/C ain't been workin' for months an' it's over a hundred degrees outside..."

The nurse brought me a fresh glass of ice water.

"We didn't think you was ever gonna wake up, honey pie. You been sleepin' for two weeks, an' Doctor Williams ain't got no idea why."

It was hot, a smothering, humid heat. New Orleans smack in the middle of Chicago. Chokichi was there that morning when I woke up. And he told me everything. I'd been at the University of Illinois Hospital for two weeks already.

Nurse Baumfree asked Chokichi to leave the room so she could ask me some questions. About, no doubt, the "device" implanted in my ribcage—and the heart that was no longer there. I gave her the contact information of the heart surgeon who'd performed the surgery. Then I asked for a glass of water.

She left, promising that she'd be back later for routine tests. They were intrigued by my condition and were attributing my coma, for the time being, to the experimental nature of the surgery. Obviously. I didn't feel ill at all, though. I was hot, yes, and not exactly in top shape on account of all the tubes they plugged into my veins, torso and temples; all those annoying machines beeping non-stop. But I wasn't in any pain, and the only thing I truly wanted was to rip out all the tubes, take off the hideous hospital gown, put on some real clothes and get the hell out of there.

"I got this at the youth hostel two days after you were admitted."

Chokichi handed me an envelope as he came back into the room.

Chokichi
Hostelling International Chicago
24 East Congress Parkway
Chicago, IL 60605
USA

"Who's it from?"
"See for yourself. It's about you, anyway."
I opened the envelope: a tiny white card, barely a few words.

Chokichi. Stay right where you are. I'm coming over.
We'll take care of Hollywood when I get there.
Saké

"You found her?"

"No. Remember how she left without telling a soul where she was going? Did you tell anyone we were in Chicago?"

"No. Did you?"

"No."

"What about the postmark?" I asked, taking back the envelope.

"Stockholm."

The envelope had indeed been postmarked by the Swedish postal service.

"I suppose all we can do now is wait for her. I'm hooked up to all kinds of machines anyway. It's not like I'm going anywhere."

Chokichi brought me a sandwich and left. I almost swallowed it whole, then threw up a few minutes later.

"You can't wolf down your food like that, darlin'. Your stomach ain't used to it no more," said Nurse Baumfree, who'd come to clean me up.

Ironically enough, after sleeping for two weeks, I was too exhausted to feel any shame. I let her change the sheets and bring me a clean gown. She unplugged some of the machines so that I could walk a little around the room.

"Be careful not to trip an' fall. Your legs is probably still asleep."

I waited until she was gone to sit up on the edge of the tiny bed. The catheter in my arm was starting to hurt. I winced as I ripped it off, then put a towel over the wound to keep it from bleeding out. I waited for a few minutes, stretched my legs a couple of times and finally stood up. I was dizzy. I managed to wobble over to the small armchair by the window and collapsed into it. I turned on the TV and flipped through the channels for a few minutes. Stupid music videos. Talk shows with guests I'd never heard of. Lots of ads for insurance companies. And that documentary on Jupiter that I'd watched recently on the Space Channel. The coincidence unsettled me, but I watched it for a third time all the same. I was too exhausted to want to do anything else. I closed my eyes, hoping to fall asleep.

The documentary was over, and I was still wide awake. An episode of *Star Trek: Deep Space Nine* had started. I turned off the TV: I've always hated Worf and O'Brien.

Nothing to read. No music. No one to talk to. That hospital, that night, made me wish I could just die. I rang. A nurse I hadn't met before came to see me. She refused to give me anything to help me sleep. "Not in your condition," she said. My condition... She brought me a copy of the *Chicago Tribune* so that I could entertain myself doing crossword puzzles. I failed miserably.

I kind of suck at crosswords—I can't name a single river in Nigeria—and realized that my knowledge of English was somewhat limited: my vocabulary doesn't include any "Manicurist's tools," and I'm at a complete loss before "Scoundrels," "Bull's League (abbr.)" and "Hullabaloo." I lay down, got up, went back to bed, and my desire to die only grew stronger. I read the newspaper from cover to cover, including the classifieds and the obituaries. Then I rang again. The same nurse came to see me, a bit less eager this time.

"Honey, you have to stop beeping me if it's not an emergency. I have other patients to tend to, you know..."

I asked her if any of her patients might be awake and available to have tea or coffee with me. She looked at me like I was a moron and left the room without bothering to answer. She should work on her bedside manner, I yelled after her. She didn't turn back to comment.

At that moment, the window shattered into pieces and a tiny rock bounced on the floor before me, stopping in front of the bathroom door. I went to pick it up. It was scorching hot. I threw it on the bed. At this rate, I thought, I'll soon be so used to meteorites that I'll watch them crash without batting an eye. But this time it felt different. Something else had happened: an explosion had knocked me to the ground. I crawled to the window across the broken glass, scraping my knees and elbows. I pulled myself up onto the ledge to take a look outside. Part of the parking lot had been blasted off on the rooftop opposite our building. A car exploded, and the fire spread quickly. The firemen intervened straight away, as did the stone-faced nurse. She came to help me back to bed, and she disinfected my scratches and wounds. A janitor quickly came to sweep the floor, and I was transferred to another room. No windows this time. Like I was being punished for bringing heaven's wrath down upon myself or something. It was six in the morning when I was finally left alone in my new room, with my copy of the *Chicago Tribune* and the pebble I'd managed to pocket without anyone noticing.

Chokichi came by around eight thirty with the latest news and my things from the hostel.

"They say this comet is heading straight into the sun. It's so close now that the frozen part in the middle is evaporating, exploding all over the place into pieces of rock. The rock just entered the atmosphere, which started a meteor shower. Most of them burn up before they crash, but some fall to Earth, like the one that just hit Chicago."

"I got a chunk of it last night," I said, handing him my little piece of comet.

Chokichi examined it for a moment. A small, dented piece of rock.

"It looks just like any other pebble."

"Are you disappointed?"

"A little, to be honest."

"Me too. It's not the end of the world just yet."

He handed me back the rock, which I hid under my pillow.

"I didn't sleep at all last night. And not because of the explosion. I was awake when it happened. The night nurse hates me and she won't do anything for the pain."

"What do you need?"

"Anything. I just want to sleep."

"I'll see what I can do."

Chokichi got up and left the room. I used the time alone to take a longer look at my pebble. It had seemed yellow the night before. Now it was no more interesting than a regular piece of cracked black rock, the kind you can find anywhere. I turned on the TV in frustration. A 24-hour news network covered the story three times in the space of ten minutes. No victims had been reported: the meteor that destroyed the cars on the rooftop opposite had only hit the administrative wing of the hospital, which lay empty at night. NASA had provided images of the comet, and a scientist was explaining the phenomenon in layman's terms to the broadcasters. They looked dumbstruck, verging on distressed. The expert was telling people not to worry: it was highly unlikely that more comet fragments would hit the ground. The one that had totalled the cars was twenty-five centimetres in diameter. I looked at mine: a couple of centimetres at most. The report ended on a message to amateur astronomers: the meteor shower would last a few nights longer, so this was the perfect time to get out their telescopes and bring the kids to the national park to take in the show.

It was the biggest meteor shower in living memory.

Chokichi came back a half-hour or so later with a bottle of pills.

"Only one before bed. Two if you want to sleep through the night *and* the next day."

I asked him how he'd managed to get them.

"Like a true Japanese, I summoned my inner ninja."

He put on a dramatic face and tried to pull some ninja moves. I laughed.

"Actually, it was a breeze: I walked the halls until I came across a nurse doing her round, pushing a cart. I waited for her to go into a patient's room and looked through what she was toting around. And I got myself a little bonus..."

Out of his pocket, he produced another bottle containing fifty or so tiny pink tablets.

"Morphine," he said. "To help with our cashflow."

I thanked him, and he smiled.

"Don't mention it. You'd do the same for me."

He leaned over the bed and gave me a long kiss. Then he got up and left the room.

"I'll be back late this afternoon," he said without turning back.

I popped a sleeping pill, lay down and pulled the covers up, waiting for the sandman to come.

Hollywood

UNDERGROUND POEM #19

writing from nowhere
from the dark recesses of my shadow
that I keep pacing to find
bliss of the never-ending kind

Montauk

HOLLYWOOD ISN'T IN THE LIVING ROOM, the kitchen or the den. The small bedroom is empty. Xavier slips on his shoes, goes back into the main bedroom to grab a wool blanket and walks out onto the porch. Shooting stars tear across the black sky, their flashes periodically lighting up the night. He sits down on the chipped wood of the old porch and bundles himself in the blanket. He watches the sky and listens to the sea.

As the night fades, his surroundings quickly take shape. First, Xavier can make out the dunes just in front of the house. Then, the tall grass swaying gently in the early morning breeze. Not a cloud in sight. And Xavier still can't sleep. He gets up and walks under a blue sky to the sea. He takes off his shoes and socks and rolls his pants up to the knees. Although the water is freezing, he moves forward through the ripples until his pants are wet. The ocean spray bathes his face. He keeps going.

Before long the water reaches his neck and the salt stings his eyes. He has trouble keeping his balance; his clothes, heavy with water, pull him down. He lets himself fall onto his back. He is chilled to the bone. The surf quickly sweeps him back onto the beach. There's no point in suffering like this, but he doesn't move, aware of how stupid he's being. The cold empties his mind and puts his thoughts at rest. Then the pain becomes unbearable. He flips over and crawls a little, trying to stand up. Once he gets his legs under him, he heads back to the house as fast as he can. He strips off his clothes on the porch before he even makes it through the door. He goes straight into the living room, naked, freezing, dripping, covered in sand. He makes a fire and wraps himself up in the rug.

That is how Hollywood finds him, in the middle of the afternoon, when he wakes up on the living room sofa.

"You seem rested," Xavier says, coughing.

"I've stopped trying to understand," Hollywood replies.

Xavier stands without thinking of concealing his nakedness.

"I'm going to take a shower and get dressed. I'll be back."

Hollywood watches him leave the room. He, too, gets up. He sits down at the piano, hits a few notes, then snaps the cover closed: he can't get a single tune out of it. He shouts over to Xavier, who's just gotten out of the shower.

"You hungry? We could go into town. Maybe the stores are open today."

Xavier walks into the living room wearing a polo shirt, golf slacks and white loafers with a tiny green crocodile on the outer edge. His hair is still wet, but he looks better than when Hollywood first found him in the living room.

"At least these guys know how to dress!"

"Yeah, if you like the rich douchey look..."

They both laugh.

"OK. Yeah, I'm hungry. Just let me grab a jacket from the front hall closet and a couple hundreds from our stash, and I'm ready."

Hollywood ties his shoes and slips on a jacket as well. They head out, locking the door behind them. It's more a reflex than a precaution. They haven't seen a living soul since they arrived.

The streets are empty. So are the houses. Nobody's in the restaurants. Or the stores. They're walking through a ghost town. The only thing they hear is the sound of their own footsteps. It's warm: about ten degrees. The sun is beating down. The grocery store isn't locked: they walk in and go through the aisles, haphazardly throwing items into the big cart that they'll bring back to the beach house. They slip a few bills into the open cash drawer. Hollywood leaves a note for whoever finds it first. Then they set off with their shopping cart. Since no cars have driven through for some time, a dusting of snow still covers the ground. The cart's wheels get caught in the snow now and then, but they keep moving at a good pace. Xavier stops in front of the pharmacy.

"I need something to help me sleep. I won't be able to otherwise."

They run up against a locked door. Hollywood knocks three times: nothing happens. He sits down on the low concrete wall to the right of the entrance.

"What do we do now?"

Xavier doesn't answer. He walks through the deserted parking lot, wandering around for a few minutes. Then he takes a step back, gathering momentum, and starts to run. He charges straight into the glass door, making contact with a thud but not breaking it. Xavier crumples to the ground, his face twisted by the pain ripping through his shoulder. Hollywood gets up.

"You OK?" he asks, worried.

"Yeah," Xavier mutters.

He gets to his feet, massaging his shoulder and arm.

"I thought it would work. Like in the movies."

"In the movies they use fake glass made of sugar."

Xavier starts to laugh, despite the pain.

"It's almost never like in the movies, in real life. That's what I'm realizing lately. It doesn't bother you, that we're constantly being lied to?"

Hollywood pulls a face.

"I don't know. I never really thought about it..."

He gets up and plants a foot on one of the wall's concrete slabs. It wobbles. He looks at Xavier, and they exchange a smile. Hollywood picks up the concrete slab and hurls it with all his might into the pharmacy door. It shatters, triggering a deafening alarm. Hollywood nudges the hole with his toe, brushing away the bits of glass still clinging to the doorframe. He goes first, ducking to avoid getting hurt. Xavier is right behind him.

The lights came on inside the second the alarm went off. Hollywood and Xavier zip up and down the aisles. The noise tears through their eardrums and they walk with their hands over their ears to protect themselves from the blare. Hollywood spots the sleeping pills behind the counter. He stuffs a few boxes into his pockets while Xavier grabs the first painkiller he finds— anything to soothe his bruised shoulder.

"Do we need anything else?" he yells.

"Cold medicine. Always a good idea. I'll take care of it."

Hollywood hops over the counter and heads to the cough syrup display.

"I'll grab the hard stuff!" yells Xavier.

He quickly rummages through the drawers and shelves, looking for familiar names, drugs he's pitched in what seems like another lifetime. He skips over some, since neither of them suffers from liver disease or chronic constipation. He cradles the boxes of OxyContin he finds in a drawer, then hesitates. He closes the drawer without taking anything.

"I can't handle all the noise. I'll wait for you outside," Hollywood tells him as he passes.

Xavier turns, pulls the drawer open again, then kicks it shut. He grabs two boxes of an antidepressant that he self-prescribed when he came back from Bilbao. He meets Hollywood outside. They throw the loot into the shopping cart and hurry away, even though no one has appeared yet outside the vandalized store.

Twenty minutes later they're at the house. They put away their spoils, and Hollywood heats up a pizza in the oven.

They have already established their routines. Xavier wipes down the porch table and sets two places. He opens a bottle of wine, letting the alcohol breathe, and lights a fire in the living room.

"This time the house will be warm when we come back in."

Hollywood puts a record on the turntable and cranks up the speakers before coming out. They sit outside and watch the sun set while the pizza cooks in the oven. They listen in silence to an opera chosen at random from the collection. *The Bloody Nun* by Charles Gounod, a title Hollywood found funny.

They eat quickly; the temperature has plummeted since the sun disappeared. They return to the living room without clearing the table. Hollywood chooses another record and they listen, their faces to the fire, as they empty a second, then a third bottle of wine.

"One time I went four nights without sleeping," says Xavier. "On the fifth night, my eyelids began twitching and I started to hallucinate. I called a friend and he brought me to the ER. I was nineteen, I think. I didn't know anything about drugs back then; I'd just started university and I didn't even know what a pharmaceutical rep was. The ER doctor prescribed me a strong sleeping pill that was supposed to knock me out cold within minutes. We went back to my apartment and I took it. We watched a movie on TV. It kept feeling like I was on the verge of sleep, but every time my head would fall onto my chest or back against the sofa, I'd wake up. I went to lie down in my bed. I left the living room to my friend, who'd promised to stay until the next morning. I wanted to make sure I'd wake up if I fell asleep. I wanted to sleep, not *die*. I tossed and turned in bed for at least an hour, then woke my friend who was sleeping on the sofa. We went back to the hospital. We waited at least two hours, even though no one was there. The same doctor was on duty. It must have been close to 6 a.m. when he finally saw me. He looked at me like I was bothering him and asked me what I was still doing there. I explained. He told me I was being dumb, that I should just take another pill, that I didn't have to come back to the ER for that. Back in my friend's car, I took two more pills; the doctor had put it into my head that it was OK to adjust the dosage myself. I blacked out, woke up forty-eight hours later. My friend was sleeping in the bed with me. He explained that he'd had to get me out of the car and drag me up to my third-floor apartment, that he'd taken off my clothes and put me to bed and kept watch for two days to make sure I was still breathing. He hadn't let himself drift off for more than twenty minutes at a stretch. He was exhausted, but I felt great. Like nothing had happened, except for a mealy taste in my mouth, which disappeared the second I brushed my teeth. We went to my friend's place. I drove his car, since he was too tired. He crawled into bed, and I left him. I went back to my house, studied for an exam, went on with my life since everything had gone back to normal. I started taking two pills at night before bed, and I'd nod off almost immediately. The following Friday, I still hadn't heard from my friend. He hadn't come to class all week. I thought it was from the two days he'd spent watching over me. I wanted to talk to him, but his phone had been disconnected. I went over to his place; his mother opened the door. They were emptying out his apartment. He'd died in his sleep. Overdosed on the sleeping pills the doctor had prescribed me—he'd lifted some while I was out cold. He'd died instead of me, because I hadn't been there to watch over him."

Hollywood doesn't say anything. He pours the rest of the wine into Xavier's glass.

"I know a lot more about drugs today because of my job, and I know I'm not always careful, but I can't help it: I can't control the pull I feel when I see a bottle of

141

pills. Like it's been burned into me that swallowing a pill makes everything better. I know it's dumb. And dangerous. It pisses me off when I see other people behaving that way. Like my colleague Antony, who thinks we're helping out humanity by being drug reps. Shifting the responsibility like that, it's crap. Today almost everyone is addicted to some drug or another, and there's a pill for just about everything. Every year pharmaceutical companies are making bank. And I'm supporting the industry through my work. It's disgusting, but I don't know what else to do. I was planning to quit before New York came up. And then I find myself here, and I don't know how..."

Xavier stands up.

"Well," he says. "There's a bottle of sleeping pills on the counter in the washroom. Just take one. I swear I won't take more than one either."

He goes to the kitchen and pours himself a glass of water. Hollywood still hasn't moved.

"Goodnight," Xavier calls out, closing the bedroom door.

This time, Hollywood decides to sleep in the small bedroom. He pours a glass of water, undresses and throws back the sleeping pill Xavier said he should take. He crawls under the covers. He added a few logs to the fire on his way out of the living room and now the house is warm. He listens to the creaking of the walls and the silence all around him. Then he falls asleep.

Xavier

I "WOKE UP" A MONTH LATER IN A HOSPITAL ROOM with a view over Greenpoint, a Brooklyn neighbourhood on the other side of the East River. I'd missed my appointment with Gia, of course. And been fired by Pullman. I learned all of this from talking to the guy in the next bed and from the countless voicemails left by Pullman, Antony and the sick colleague I was supposed to replace.

The whole thing was a huge pain.

A doctor came to see me as soon as the nurse on duty realized I was awake. He wanted to keep me under observation for at least a week given that my mysterious "coma" was still undiagnosed. But since I was feeling great—mainly thanks to the lovely nurse who'd taken care to move my arms and legs every day so the muscles wouldn't atrophy—and since I knew how much a hospital stay in the United States would run me, I arranged to be discharged the next day.

I spent the whole day in rehab, walking on a treadmill under the watchful eye of a physiotherapist. I called Pullman, who hurled a stream of abuse at me over the phone until I told him I'd just woken up from a month-long coma. He changed his tune right away and asked if I was feeling better.

"Cut the crap," I told him. "Consider this my resignation 'letter.'"

He suggested I think on it before making such a big move. But since I'd already been fired and the papers had been sent to my apartment in Toronto, I told him not to worry or bother changing the information printed on the letter dismissing me, just to give me a small severance package so that I could pay the hospital bill and still come out OK. We agreed on two months' salary, along with a formal promise on my end not to take legal action for unfair dismissal. He transferred me to the HR secretary, who recorded my consent in my file and wished me a good day.

I called Antony. He'd been worried, of course.

"I know," I told him. "You left me at least twenty voicemails."

"So, when will you be back?"

"Tomorrow, on Amtrak. Want to pick me up at Union Station?"

"*T'arrives à quelle heure?*"

"8 p.m."

"That means you won't be here before noon the day after tomorrow, at best."

"Why's that?" I asked.

"The fucking snow, man."

I looked out of the window. There was snow, all right. The East River was frozen, not a single boat was out. I saw cars on the bridges, everything seemed normal for this time of year. Then I remembered: I'd been asleep for a month, so it was April now. Springtime. But New York was still sporting a white overcoat.

"It snowed every day in March," Antony told me. "This shit isn't over yet."

He brought me up to speed. The snow removal crews in Calgary, Edmonton, Regina, Saskatoon and Winnipeg had been sent to back up those in Toronto, Ottawa, Montreal and Quebec City. Crews that weren't busy clearing the snow that was constantly being dumped on Canada had crossed the border to lend a hand to struggling New England cities. It hadn't warmed up; the temperature was holding steady below freezing, which kept the snow from melting and crippled certain activities. Among other things, the trains weren't running on time since freight cars were stuck on poorly cleared stretches or covered in snowdrifts. On the coldest nights, engines just broke down. Meteorologists had told North America's eastern residents to prepare for another few months of the endless winter. According to their calculations, it was very possible that summer vacations would be spent on snowy beaches. It was the same in Western Europe. Over a hundred thousand deaths had been recorded in France, with even more in Spain and Portugal. England's toll wasn't quite as devastating, but many there had fled to former colonies—Australia, India, the West Indies—to escape the bone-chilling cold and damp.

"Fuck. I'm sick of it," I said.

"I know, man. Hang in there. Anyway, *on n'a pas vraiment le choix*. Unless you're game to skip out and go live somewhere else. As for me, the lady won't move, so I'm stuck here. At least I got to enjoy Aruba."

He told me about his trip. I wanted to die. Luckily, a nurse came by and reminded me that I wasn't allowed to use my cellphone in the hospital, and that I was being irresponsible and whatnot. I hung up.

I still had to reach Gia.

The number you have dialled is not in service.

I kicked the radiator. The guy in the next bed snickered. I looked daggers at him, but that only made him laugh harder.

"When are you going to die?" I asked him in French, thinking he wouldn't understand.

"Soon, *si tout va bien*," he replied.

I froze, shocked.

"Yes, I'm French and I'm going to die."

He began to tell me his story. I went over and sat in the little chair on his side of the room. A crank who'd become so obsessed with Hervé Guibert that he'd tried to emulate his writing, in vain, and then his life, with more success: he'd picked up AIDS voluntarily by having unprotected sex with loads of boys—some HIV positive, some not—and had refused treatment so he could die as young as possible *in tribute to his idol* who had lived before the miracle drug. Raph (that was his name) had collapsed on a Manhattan street while retracing Guibert's route during one of his visits to the *Caput mundi*. After an emergency transfer to the hospital, he'd been diagnosed with *Pneumocystis* pneumonia. He had left the hospital, returning to wander the city streets and spend his nights infecting East Village barebackers. Since he refused medication, he didn't have long to live. He'd been dragged to the hospital by his lover *du jour*, another crank who thought he was Truman Capote but who had enough common sense not to leave his friend to die like a stray cat in a dark alley. He spoke for a while, about an hour, spitting up blood every other sentence. He told me about a whole bunch of things I'd rather not remember. His monologue didn't leave room for me to get a word in, which was good considering I wouldn't have known what to say.

I was discharged the next morning, as planned. I gathered my things and took a taxi to Penn Station. The train left on time, but we didn't arrive in Toronto until 4 a.m. Antony had been waiting since midnight, not knowing what time the train would pull in.

"Bro! Real happy to see you!"

He hugged me. I was excited to see him, too. A familiar face. To my surprise—and to Antony's, for that matter—I burst into tears in his arms. He started laughing.

"No worries! Let it out, man."

Xavier

My days don't belong to me. I haven't slept since I got back and I don't feel tired. I watch movies all night without getting into them. Even the ones I'm watching for the hundredth time, the ones that usually pick me up, have no effect. It's cold out. It snows every other day. The nights are freezing. I drink beer and eat burgers. I wait for something to happen.

I got out my notebook again, tried a few sketches. I can't manage anything meaningful. I go round in circles. Even words go round in circles.

Hollywood

IT HAPPENED AGAIN, except this time, I didn't wake up in a hospital, but in an apartment I didn't know. I was alone; I explored the one-bedroom, leaning on chairs and other pieces of furniture so that I wouldn't fall. My legs were still shaky.

It was hot and stuffy. The curtains had been drawn, probably to stop the sun from making the air—already damp and sticky from the heat—even warmer. There wasn't much in the apartment, but enough to lead me to believe I was living there with Saké and Chokichi.

By the look of things, the couch was being used as Saké's bed, dressing room and headquarters. An old blue leather suitcase was bursting with extravagant wigs and sunglasses. The ground was littered with scarves, skirts, nylons, tank tops, dresses, makeup, bedsheets and a pillow. On the table I found a pocket mirror, a tube of bright red lipstick, a tissue with a big fat kiss on it, a dirty cup

149

with a few sips of cold coffee still in it and an ashtray chock full of cigarette butts. A book was lying on the coffee table: *J'aime et je cuisine le concombre*, by Aglaé Blin. I went straight to the kitchen and looked into the fridge to confirm my suspicions: it was filled with virtually nothing but cucumbers, along with a tub of *crème fraîche*, green onions and a bundle of fresh mint. One of Saké's whims, I thought to myself. Her latest obsession.

I continued exploring. On the kitchen counter there was a coffee machine, a fan and a 1986 phone book for Madison, Alabama. I pulled back the curtains and looked outside. Was that Madison, Alabama, out there? Could be. I drew the curtains: the sun was brutal. The clock on the microwave said 7:00 p.m. I paused to think about the time, date and place before I went on inspecting the apartment. A pack of cigarettes was lying next to the stove. I brought one to my lips and lit one of the two burners. I moved the tip closer to the blue flame. It caught right away. I turned off the gas.

I went back to my room. My things were there, so I rushed over to my bag and took out my iPod. It had been too long. I pressed the earbuds into my ears and sank into bed as the music started. I closed my eyes. Happiness overload. I couldn't face the outside world and be looking at it at the same time. I had to make a choice.

Chokichi woke me up. I took out my earbuds and sat up.
"What time is it?" I asked.
"8 p.m."

I'd barely slept an hour, and nothing had happened. Chokichi lay down on his back next to me. His arm against mine. I stayed still.

"This time, you were in a coma for a little over a week. Saké came to Chicago. She knew where to find us. And she got this crazy idea that we should kidnap you from the hospital and bring you here. That's why she rented the apartment in the first place, so the three of us could hide out here. I think she picked that up in a movie or something. I tried to convince her that it would never work—not in a million years—but she kept insisting, so we spent the night plotting and scheming, and then we tried our luck."

"You *kidnapped* me from the hospital?"

Chokichi laughed, throwing his head back.

"Ah! That girl, she's really something else!"

"Where is she now, come to think of it?"

"Fucking hell... That girl! They're paying her to sing the US national anthem for this all-girls softball league."

"And what day is it?"

"April 29."

I sighed.

"It must be a lot to take in, eh?" said Chokichi. "There's no hurry."

He took my iPod and began to search for something.

"I started listening to some music while I was watching over you. I really like this," he said, showing me the cover of Joni Mitchell's *Court and Spark*.

I smiled.

"Watching you sleep isn't all it's cracked up to be. Plus Saké confiscated all my gear. But in the end it wasn't so bad; I could listen to your music. That album is my absolute favourite."

We talked about Joni Mitchell for a few minutes. My mouth was dry. After all, I'd just been asleep for over a week. I got up to get a glass of water, but this time my legs were having none of it. I fell over the bed. My head landed on Chokichi's stomach.

He laughed, sending my head bobbing up and down. I started to laugh too. He leaned down and kissed me. I closed my eyes. He ruffled my hair with one hand. Then the apartment door flung open and we heard Saké yell: "Chokichi! I'm starving! Would you peel a few cucumbers and make *gazpacho*?"

Chokichi scrambled up. My head fell back onto the mattress. I heard a thud: Saké had just tossed her bag on the table. Chokichi went to the kitchen and told her I was awake. She ran to my room right away.

"Yo, Holly! Glad to see you back. How do you feel?"

She kissed me on the cheeks and gave me a hug.

"OK, I think."

"You *think*?"

"I'm just not sure, is all. I've been awake for a couple of hours, at most. And I'm scared I might pass out again if I fall back to sleep."

As I spoke, an awful cramp tore through my ribcage. I winced and breathed in through clenched teeth. Chokichi and Saké jumped over to help.

"I'm all right. It's just a cramp."

I got up and walked to the bathroom. I locked the door and lay down in the bathtub. I counted to 1,276, then got up and came back out. Both of them were at the kitchen table, smoking.

"I want one," I said, sitting down next to them.

"You sure?" asked Saké.

"I *want* one," I repeated.

She passed me a cigarette. Chokichi gave me a light.

"Do we have anything to drink?" I asked.

Chokichi got three glasses out of the cupboard. Then he opened the freezer to look for ice, and filled the glasses halfway with big cubes. In the meantime, Saké went to the living-room section of the pint-sized apartment and came back holding a lime and a bottle of rum. She cut the lime into three pieces, put one into each glass and poured rum over the ice, filling our glasses to the brim. We drank. Then we ate cold cucumber soup.

Saké had brought along—all the way to this tiny one-bedroom she'd found online—an old stereo and a collection of tapes from a Chicago second-hand store. She rummaged through the box and put on *Kiss Me Deadly*, by Generation X. Before she pressed play, she told us how the group first got together. She talked about Billy Idol and announced that the first song on the album, *Dancing With Myself*, was one of her "all-time faves." That's what she said. She cranked up the volume and pushed on the little triangle.

She didn't come back to sit with us. Nope. She tossed her shoes on the sofa, hitched up her dress over her hips and climbed onto the table. She started dancing, screaming the lyrics at the top of her lungs. I drank my glass in one gulp and joined her. Chokichi did the same. All three of us were soon standing on the table, dancing as if our very lives depended on it. We didn't move our feet, though, because we didn't have much space. Eventually Saké started jumping up and down, clearly drunk, lost in the music. One of the table legs gave way under our weight, followed by the other three. We fell flat on the floor, in an infernal din of cracked melamine, clanging metal and cries of shock and pain. Our downstairs neighbour banged on the ceiling. I was laughing so hard I couldn't move, like I was paralyzed with joy at feeling my whole body ache from the fall. Saké pulled herself up, adjusted her wig, dress and nylons, and sat down on one of the two chairs that had survived our fall. I stayed lying on the debris, beside Chokichi, still shaking and crying from laughter. Chokichi finally got up to refill our glasses.

"Hit me again," said Saké. "To the brim!"

"Coming right up."

I calmed down and wiped my eyes.

"So now will you tell me how you guys kidnapped me from the hospital?" I asked.

"I need a drink first," said Saké.

Chokichi handed her the first glass and put the other two on the counter. I got up. Saké was already drinking, on her third or fourth sip. Her drink was gone in no time. She wiped her mouth.

"Aaaah..."

Chokichi clinked glasses with me. We drank. I didn't down my drink, though. I wanted to have some left to survive the story I was about to hear.

"Actually, what surprises me most is how easy it was to pull off," Saké began. "I thought stealing a corpse would be harder."

I almost choked on my drink.

"A *corpse*?"

"Sorry, I meant a *body*. It's just that you didn't help much with the actual 'kidnapping,' so the whole corpse thing seemed about right."

Saké rose from her chair and turned off the lights. Chokichi lit some candles he'd gotten out of the cupboard. Those two were acting as if they shared one mind, like they no longer needed words to communicate.

Saké sat down and went on. "First, I rented the apartment. I was looking for something that wouldn't be close to Chicago, but not too far away either, so we could get there the same day. So I took a look at a map, found this little spot and skimmed through the classifieds on the Internet. I took the bus over, met with the landlord, gave him a deposit and got the keys. I went back to Chicago, met up with Chokichi and the two of us put the rest of our plan together."

She paused, refilled her glass and took a sip of rum.

"We had to rent a car, preferably a van, but a plain-looking one, so we wouldn't draw attention to ourselves. I let Chokichi take care of the van, while I looked for costumes and worked out the onsite logistics. But I'll let Chokichi tell you that part."

Chokichi cleared his throat.

"I thought it best to work undercover, on the sly, so I wouldn't leave a paper trail, like in the movies, you know? So instead of going to a car rental where I'd have to show my passport and credit card, I called up a friend in Montreal. He knows people, so he gave me the number of a guy who recommended another guy, and so on, until I got the address of this mechanic—a small-time crook, I'm told—in La Grange Park, a suburb of Chicago. I went over to his shop and we met up in the backyard, where he fixes cars for friends and people he knows. I told him I was looking to rent something nondescript for a decent price. I thought he'd try to sell me a van with an exterminator's logo, like in the movies, right? But no. He shows me this battered wreck he put back together, something ridiculous: a small yellow school bus. Bright yellow. 'People never suspect a school bus,' he says. 'They always assume they've got every right to be there. They're school buses, for cryin' out loud.' And he had a point. I mean, my imagination is more likely to run wild if I see an exterminator's van parked on the street than if I see a school bus. Plus there'd be lots of room in the bus for us to move your body and our things. I traded him some of the morphine for the bus. It didn't cost us a cent."

Then they told me how Saké spent days staking out my floor at the hospital to decide when they should go ahead with their plan. How she got uniforms so that she and Chokichi could pose as nurses. And they finally came to the *pièce de résistance*, the crux of the matter: my kidnapping. They stole a stretcher from the ambulance entrance, brought it up to my room and, when the floor was empty, unplugged me, put me on the stretcher and ran full speed to the parking lot, where the bus was waiting. They loaded the stretcher onto the bus, started the engine and drove for ten hours straight to Madison, Alabama, only stopping for gas. They put me in the bedroom, and Chokichi watched over me virtually night and day. Saké got rid of the uniforms, the bus and anything else that might have incriminated them. She got hired to sing the national anthem for an amateur sports club and started wearing wigs, dressing like an exotic dancer and living on a diet of cucumbers and rum.

"I feel great. Like a woman. Healthy. Never hungry. And always drunk. I wouldn't have it any other way!"

She took a timely sip of rum.

"You should try it: a little black dress, a pair of nylons, red high heels, a purple wig and lots of eyeliner. A swig of rum in the morning, cold cucumbers for lunch, a couple more glasses of rum in the afternoon, then off to belt out the *Star-Spangled Banner*, pissed drunk before a bunch of little girls dressed in beige who want nothing more than to hit a softball. It's full-on cathartic, really puts it all in perspective. It helps you see the world a little more clearly."

She burst out laughing.

"I'm so damned drunk. Time for bed." She blew us a few kisses. "Goodnight, boys!"

Hollywood

like a wave upon the rocks
after a long walk
inside your twilight eyes
merely red and orange stains
for whoever doesn't understand

Xavier

I HAVEN'T SLEPT since I got back to Toronto. I don't need to. Sleep doesn't come, and I'm not tired.

It stopped snowing, but the air is still icy. One night, while I was going round in circles, the lights went out. I looked out the window: the whole city was plunged into darkness. I'd never seen Toronto like that before. It was twenty below, but I bundled up and went out.

The snow crunched under my feet. Cars were stopped any which way in the street and people were panicking, trying to get them to start up again. They tried to use their cellphones or warm themselves with cigarette lighters, but nothing worked: cars wouldn't start, cellphones weren't responding, lighter flames were blown out by the cold wind. You'd have thought generators would turn the lights back on in places, but nothing happened. Winter had paralyzed us. And it would be May in a few days.

Then I looked up.

I'd never seen anything so beautiful in my life.

It was like I was looking at the sky for the first time, the sky that our ancestors would have seen before industrialization. It made me realize how the marvel of colour and light could have fascinated them so much. There was something everywhere I looked: a constellation, a cloud of red, purple, orange or blue dots. At last I saw the Milky Way, the long glowing trail arching across the sky. And I noticed the shooting stars, winking on and off after having run their course. I counted twenty, thirty, then lost count because they were moving too fast and there were too many at once.

The city lights came back on, the cars decided to start, the cellphones began working again. I went home.

A geomagnetic storm, they explained on TV, caused by a powerful solar flare.

::

The next morning, I got a text message from Gia. *meet @ sheraton lounge, floor 43, ask for club room to get in. saturday 8 p.m. enjoy the view while u wait.*

Two days to get ready.

::

I walked up to the reception desk. I was offered a suite with a king bed on the thirty-eighth floor. I paid. I went up to the Club lounge. It was almost 8 p.m. They were serving appetizers. I ordered a martini and went to sit by the south side window. I sipped my drink as I listened to the music and admired the view. An old album was playing, a mix of jazz and country that sounded half-cabaret, half-folk. Strange, but incredibly beautiful. You could hear the dust of the old LP over the music. A female singer with a deep, gravelly voice was crooning and scatting, then began belting out: *"Will someone remember me?"* A giant shiver ran through me, as if I'd suddenly found myself on the roof and was exposed to the icy wind blowing over the monstrous city. I closed my eyes. When I opened them again, it was snowing over Toronto. From my chair, I could see the CN Tower and the skyscrapers of the financial district: BMO, Scotiabank, TD. The buildings formed a wall that prevented me from seeing the lake only a few streets over. I closed my eyes again and focused on the singer's voice. A dark voice, a voice of dust, cigarettes and scotch. A voice from an old record.

A bar employee touched my shoulder.

"Sir, I have a message for you."

He had roused me from my thoughts, but I acted as if he hadn't startled me.

"Thank you."

I took the envelope from his gloved hand.

Xavier,

You must learn to forget me. I only passed through your life like you passed through mine. I already have someone who shares my days. I reserve you for the extra-

162

ordinary. Don't look for me; I will find you when the time is right. In the meantime, get some rest and enjoy the beautiful view. You look adorable by the window.

Paç fat!
Gia

I turned around. Nobody was behind me. I crumpled the note with the envelope into a ball and threw it on the ground. I was sure of only one thing: I had to leave town.

Then a window on the north side exploded with a crash. I flung myself to the floor and rolled under a table to safety.

Xavier

I looked up "paç fat" in a dictionary online. It means "good luck" in Albanian. Good luck with what?

A real estate agency took charge of my apartment. I kept only what I could take with me. I bought a new notebook: new life, new notebook. But I don't know where to go. I've been at the airport for two days already. I haven't decided where to begin this new life.

I put the pebble that shattered the window of the 43rd floor of the Sheraton in my suitcase, in a cotton sock that I stuffed in the toe of a shoe, to make sure the X-rays don't pick it up.

In the meantime, while I'm still deciding, I watch the people passing by me and I draw them in my new notebook, trying to sketch the idea that I'm the focal point of a movie speeding by, the heart and soul of a silent film, even if I'm not doing a single thing.

Hollywood

"ARE YOU OK?" Chokichi asked after I'd tossed and turned at least ten times over.

"I can't sleep."

"Are you scared?"

"No. It's just not happening. I can't get to sleep."

We were lying next to each other on a mattress on the floor. An orange glimmer was piercing through a corner of the window, faintly lighting the room. I tossed again, turning to lie on my back. My leg touched Chokichi's. I didn't mean for it to happen; it just did. The mattress wasn't very wide. But I didn't move my leg. And Chokichi didn't budge. I could hear him breathing. Nothing was going on. Madison was a quiet town. A car drove by every now and then. Chokichi was breathing faster and faster. If I had a heart, I guess I would've heard it beating.

I heard a rustle under the sheets. Felt a slight pressure on my leg. Then Chokichi propped himself up,

pushed back the covers and lay down over me, strad-
dling my hips, pushing his stomach against mine. He
kissed me furiously.

I let him. I took off his shirt. He took off mine. He
nibbled my earlobes, licked my chest.

That's how it all started.

I was sticky with sweat. The air smelled of lechery.
Chokichi was trying to catch his breath. We were in
bed next to each other, backs to the wall, knees to our
chests. I stayed quiet, looking down, eyes fixed on the
hardwood floor, on the small pile of clothes we'd tossed
there.

"Makes you feel kinda weird, huh?"

"Yeah," I answered.

I felt a sting in the pit of my stomach. A cramp tore
through my ribcage. I felt flustered. A delicious, painful
feeling.

"Me too," said Chokichi.

Neither of us moved.

"There you have it. Your movie scene." I said. I had
tears running from my eyes, but I wasn't crying.

::

I spent twenty minutes in the shower with no intention
of coming out. I let the water run over my head and the
rest of my body. My hands were still shaking.

Hollywood

UNDERGROUND POEM #24

you will say it's raining out
and I will say nothing

there is someone
out there
whom I can hear no more

Part three

Xavier

IN THE END, for lack of a better idea, I opted for the most unlikely destination: a place where I could spend all my time in a hotel room without feeling absurdly guilty for not getting out and seeing the sights. I chose Pittsburgh, Pennsylvania.

A one-way flight, four hours with a connection in Boston, leaving from Toronto at 6:45 a.m. and arriving at 10:50 a.m. for $436, operated jointly by Air Canada and US Airways. I'd never been to Pittsburgh; the city certainly didn't fit into my cosmogony or mythical geography. All I knew about the place was that it was home to the Penguins, even though I couldn't care less about hockey, collateral damage, I guess, from having grown up and lived in Canada all this time...

I bought a ticket, checked my bag, went through customs and then waited about thirty minutes at the gate.

The plane took off, then landed in Boston. The connection was a breeze: my checked bag went straight through. Boarding, takeoff, landing in Pittsburgh. By 11:30 a.m. I was in a taxi heading to the Westin Convention Center, just beside the Amtrak station. The Westin, since I was planning to spend an indeterminate amount of time in my room and I wanted luxury and comfort, to, you know, balance things out.

I ended up with an executive suite featuring solid wood furniture, either mahogany or walnut, draperies, living room and bedroom, one and a half baths. I had money, so I might as well spend it.

I threw my bag onto the bed and sat down on the floor. I used my phone to look up a place nearby where I could buy a laptop. I had research to do, time to kill and money to burn.

Seeing the city covered in snow made me want to cry. There's a tricky sort of happiness that comes from being idle. When we have nowhere to go and almost no hope, we leave ourselves less open to sweeping disappointments and violent despair. We swim around in a kind of twilight zone of highs and lows.

I bought a laptop and new boots, which I wore out of the store. I gave the salesperson the pleasure of throwing out my old pair, which were full of holes, shot to pieces, not far from being considered a UNESCO world heritage site. I walked into a fusion restaurant and took the computer out of its packaging at the table. I plugged it in and connected to the first unsecured wireless network I could find.

I went to the Union des artistes website and looked up Gia Kasapi in the online directory. It didn't take long to find the agency representing her. I also learned quite a bit about her: a stint with the Modern Company of the Brookline Academy of Dance in Boston; one year at Canada's National Ballet School in Toronto; a few productions in Toronto, Montreal and New York as part of the *corps de ballet*; graduated from the English program of the National Theatre School of Canada in Montreal five years later; a handful of stage roles across Canada and the United States: Ottawa, Montreal, Victoria, Calgary, Philadelphia, New York; a black and white photo dated 2010; a list of nominations and awards; most significant role: Blanche DuBois in Tennessee Williams' *A Streetcar Named Desire,* produced in 2009 by the Centaur Theatre.

With my plate of Thai noodles in front of me, I called her agent: hello, I'd like to speak to Gia Kasapi, one of your artists. Would it be possible to make an appointment with her in the next few days? The agent said no: Gia's on tour right now. Give me your phone number and I'll pass it on.

On the way back to my room, I went on a bit of a shopping spree. In the end, I came back with a bottle of scotch, a tweed blazer with brown leather elbow patches, a frozen lasagna, a loaf of sunflower bread and a bottle of extra-strength ibuprofen for my migraine. Before leaving for Toronto I'd taken Antony's advice and thrown out all of the meds I'd stockpiled at home. The withdrawal was giving me a splitting headache; it remained to be seen if I'd be able to get to sleep without my pills—and manage it night after night.

Xavier

Night falls, with no pills to help me sleep. So it's impossible to nod off. Which means I didn't dream, because I didn't sleep.

I'm still not tired.

I'm seated in front of the window and I darken the notebook's pages, trying to reproduce what I see: the city lights reflected on the snow, the magnificent contrast between the buildings' dark shades and the almost pastel tones of the illuminated powder.

This whole time, the TV is on and a stupid movie is playing. I don't pay too much attention; I'm just reassured by the sound and the impression that my solitude is filled by the larger-than-life imaginary heroes with whom I share my room.

I keep checking my phone: no missed calls. Gia hasn't tried to get in touch.

I'd give anything for a sleeping pill. But I don't give in. Slowly, morning arrives. It's still snowing. And then it hits me: my life is looking more and more like this notebook. What I mean is: reality is merging into my own perceptions of it.

Hollywood

"WILL YOU EXPLAIN what this is really all about?"

"Meaning...?"

"Meaning why we're actually here. You told me how you brought me here and all, but that's not what I want to know. Don't you think this is completely absurd—the three of us, here, now?"

Saké took a bite of the cucumber she was holding.

"I don't know, Holly. If you think everything in life needs to have a point, a meaning, you're in for a bumpy ride, my friend."

She was right. I snatched the cucumber from her and took a big bite. It was juicy and crunchy. It calmed me down. She might be on to something with that funny diet of hers, I thought to myself.

It wasn't fear keeping me awake, I explained. I was *physically incapable* of falling asleep.

"Another of my body's eccentricities," I added. "Next thing you know, I'll grow a horn or something and I'll be off to join a circus or a band of gypsies."

"You moron!" she said, standing up. "What you need is a job. Come with me to work this afternoon: it'll take your mind off things."

So I went along to the ballpark. I was dying to see— and hear—her sing the US national anthem anyway. Saké was never the flag-waving type, not even back home.

Chokichi had left early in the morning, also looking for a job. Since I'd finally regained consciousness, and didn't seem likely to fall back into a coma any time soon, he was free to do whatever he pleased. This involved, and I quote, "making some moolah" so we could "have a good time." Whatever that meant.

I went to the softball game with Saké, only to discover that she wasn't really getting *paid* to sing the national anthem: they were giving her free hotdogs. I brought this up, because it went against just about everything I'd learned about her since I'd woken up.

"You really thought I could make it through the day on cucumbers and rum? Hell no! But franks and buns don't come cheap, you know, and if you want your hotdog to have some punch, you need a little sauerkraut, mustard, mayo, ketchup and a bunch of other toppings way beyond my budget. I told Chokichi I was getting paid so he wouldn't ask me where the rent money's coming from..."

"So... where *is* it coming from?"

She wouldn't answer right away, instead shoving a huge bite of hotdog into her mouth.

"Have one—they're free," she said with her mouth full.

I was hungry, so I made myself a hotdog. But I insisted that she answer my question.

"My folks send me money. I got an envelope in Stockholm, one in Chicago and another in Madison. I must have a GPS under my skin or something for them to be able to track me like that. In fact, that's why I left without you in the first place: I wanted to see if I could shake them off and disappear, just like they did. I don't know where they are, but they always seem to know where *I* am. I swear, it's driving me nuts."

Saké sat down in the bleachers and buried her face in her hands; she was human after all. I mean, I was worried and a bit annoyed with how little she seemed to care about her parents' disappearance, and with her lack of curiosity over where they might be. If I were her, I'd want to figure out why they left, where they were and how they always managed to know where she was.

I sat down next to her and put my arm around her shoulders. We stayed like that for about a minute, in silence. Then she got up, wiped her cheeks with the back of her hand and smiled at me.

"OK, I'm all good now. Let's forget about it." She walked over to the grill. "Want another one?"

"No thanks, I'm OK."

By the time Chokichi came home, the sun had completely disappeared below the horizon.

"It's far from glamourous, but it's better than nothing," he said, laying his orange uniform on the kitchen table.

He sat down with us, grabbed an empty glass and filled it with rum. Saké and I had already finished one bottle and started on another.

"I don't have a visa or a work permit, so they'll pay me cash. But apart from that, it's a regular job, almost legit. That should make *you* happy," he said, turning to Saké.

"It does," she said. "Better selling junkfood to fat people than scoring dope for junkies. At least... I guess."

She burst out laughing and hit her head on the table, so I started laughing too.

"I think I'm drunk."

"You *think*?"

Chokichi poured himself a second glass.

"You guys started early, by the look of things." He turned to check the clock on the microwave. "It's not even 10 yet... How much do I still have to drink to catch up?"

I paused before I answered.

"To catch up to me, only three more. I had four. But I don't know about Saké. She finished the bottle, so..."

"Yeah, I'm really drunk," she said between hiccups. "In fact, I think I better go to bed now if I don't want to be sick. Goodnight, guys!"

We wished her goodnight. She had a hard time getting up and made for the living room, leaning against the furniture and walls to keep her balance. We heard her crash on the couch; she was snoring minutes later.

Chokichi and I had a couple of drinks together and chatted about our day. So this was what 'living in society' was all about! I told him the truth about Saké: the money, the hotdogs and how she'd fallen apart on me at the softball game... He talked about his day, his new job, his lack of enthusiasm.

"Did you sleep last night?" he asked.

"No. Not a wink."

"Can you tell? Are you tired?"

"No."

We stayed up talking for a long time and managed to finish the second bottle. I was becoming more incoherent by the minute. Unable to stand, I crawled to the living room on my hands and knees to see if we'd woken Saké with our laughter. She was sleeping on her back, her mouth wide open. I guffawed, but she didn't budge.

"We're good, she's out cold!" I yelled towards the kitchen. Chokichi came in.

"What are you doing on the floor?"

"I don't know," I said. "It's more comfortable down here."

He took my hands and tried to pull me up.

"Hop on, I'll take you to bed."

He crouched down so that I could climb on his back. He stood up, and I held on to his neck. Chokichi was hammered too, which meant that he wasn't very steady on his feet. We crashed straight into a wall and stayed on the floor for a while, laughing our asses off, unable to speak. Our downstairs neighbour banged on the ceiling again, which made us laugh twice as hard. Then I managed to make my way to the bedroom on all fours, followed by Chokichi. We threw ourselves onto the bed. I wanted to listen to loud, heart-pounding music. I picked one of the albums my dad gave me. I put it on the turntable Saké had picked up at an antique store, and set the needle down right where *Black Velvet* started. It wasn't my first time listening to it, which wasn't lost on Chokichi.

"Is this Joni Mitchell, too?"

"Alannah Myles. This song rocks. Listen."

We sat on the bed, our backs to the wall. I pressed my leg against his. And neither of us moved.

When I closed my eyes, I could see the stars as if they'd been tattooed on the inside of my eyelids.

Hollywood

UNDERGROUND POEM #31

I wish I could tell you
the effulgence on these lips

Xavier

ABSOLUTELY NOTHING WAS HAPPENING. The phone hadn't rung once. Someone from housekeeping came each morning to change the towels and fill the little bottle of shampoo. I lazed about in bed until noon, even if I wasn't sleeping. I visited Pittsburgh, its bookstores and restaurants.

I bought clothes, but didn't indulge as far as to send them to the hotel laundry. From time to time, I'd take them to the Korean laundromat downtown.

While my clothes were in the machine, I sat down on a metal bench and pretended to read a collection of poetry I'd picked up second-hand. It was incredibly dull. I listened in on conversations and watched people, and it made me feel like I was taking part in something, that my existence wasn't entirely pointless because it was part of a universal program; I was part of the community.

Then, just like that, during the rinse cycle, my heart started to race. Normally, I would have taken a few pills to prevent it from going full throttle in my chest and tearing through my ribcage. But I didn't have anything on me and I'd promised Antony I'd stay clean and kick my many addictions. I took slow breaths, inhaled perhaps a little too deeply; I felt very strange, lightheaded, like I was about to pass out. I lay down on the bench. I was hot. I undid the top buttons of my shirt to let in some air. A boy came over to see me.

"Are you all right, sir?"

I said yes, then got up and left.

::

Ti je e bukur. *But there is someone else in my life, as I've said. And beyond that, there is something more crucial preventing us from being together—and it's better this way. Go back to Montauk right away, Xavier, otherwise it will be too late: the storm's only going to get worse where you are and you'll be trapped in Pittsburgh.*

Your friend,

Gia

P.S. My little boy's name is Zarik. He looks a lot like you, in a way—even if that's impossible. Unfortunately he died when he was ten days old. His little heart stopped beating. Just like that. Because these things happen.

::

185

Montauk, then. In the middle of a storm, in May. I'm fed up with the snow, but I'll drive there anyway, just for the experience. Nine hours and thirty-seven minutes, five hundred and three miles on Interstate 80, according to the Internet. We'll see how the trip goes.

Am I the only one not writing little toxic letters?

Xavier

I haven't slept a wink in two weeks. I decided to leave in three days, a Wednesday, for no particular reason. To have time to sketch the beach house from memory, in pencil. To be able to find it once I get there and compare my memories to reality. Maybe Hollywood is still there. I sure hope so.

When I'm tired of drawing, I watch the snow fall. On rare nights when the sky is clear, I watch the shooting stars. The Lyrids, Pi Puppis, Alpha Bootids, Mu Virginids and Omega Capricornids. I watch them all with fierce intensity.

May. It's still snowing.

I watch a bunch of films in my hotel room. To pass the time. I decided to devote myself to the filmography of Zooey Deschanel; I have the leisure of choosing some of my obsessions. I don't watch them in order. It all started when I caught The Hitchhiker's Guide to the Galaxy *on a sci-fi channel. Next I watched* Almost Famous *and* The Good Girl, *which I ordered off the hotel TV. Then I saw* Yes Man *and* (500) Days of Summer *and* Winter Passing *and I found out that she sings, too, so I bought three* She & Him *albums. I've been listening to them over and over ever since, especially the Christmas one because it won't stop snowing and because Zooey Deschanel's voice makes me want to cry.*

I'm trying to understand the things that escape me.

Hollywood

"DON'T YOU GET BORED?"

"Sure, sometimes. Especially at night."

We were both lying on the unmade bed. Neither of us had bothered to shake the sheets, pull up the duvet or arrange the pillows properly since we'd moved in. A few weeks ago already. Here in Madison, Alabama, the sun had been blazing hot throughout the month of May. I was slowly getting used to the value of a Fahrenheit degree. It was almost always ninety-nine degrees outside. In January, when near-zero temperatures were recorded in the past (that would be thirty-two degrees Fahrenheit, if I understood correctly), the daily average had been seventy-eight degrees. I managed to glean these figures from the daily news on TV and the newspapers Chokichi brought back after his shift at the fast-food place.

"I mean, during the day I'm all alone in here, and at night you guys are asleep, so I'm alone then too... it shouldn't change much, right? But the fact that you're right there, that I can see you and all... it bothers me a bit more."

"Hmm. I get it... I think."

"You know, I've always had trouble sleeping. I used to think that, in the end, sleep was a waste of time. You could find much more interesting things to do with your time. But now that I can make the most of my 24 hours a day, I'm starting to miss it. Sleeping puts your mind at rest. Otherwise, you just keep thinking the same thoughts over and over, and you can't take a break from yourself."

The album we were listening to came to an end. I got up to turn it over and put the needle back in place. Mahler's *Symphony No. 5*, performed by the Chicago Symphony Orchestra and conducted by Georg Solti, an old, very rare, 1970 live recording Chokichi had found at a community yard sale.

I lay back in bed. Chokichi took my hand. We stayed like that for a while, in silence, immersed in the music.

We listened to the fourth movement, Adagietto. I was focusing on nothing but the music: the violins, the harp, a discreet cough from time to time. I had tears running down my cheeks. I cried like that, quietly, throughout the piece. In my whole life, I'd never heard anything so sublime.

Then the last movement ended, and there was an endless pause before the audience clapped. A long silence during which neither of us dared to move; it felt like time had stopped. One of those moments that exist only to give you the chance to reenter your body and go back to reality.

I wiped my cheeks. Chokichi sniffled. I didn't turn to look at him. I didn't want to know if he was crying too, or just bored to death. Mahler was mine, and mine only. Then he spoke to me.

"I hope you're not mad that I read your poems."

I turned and looked him in the eye. There was a disarmingly honest look about him, and something else I couldn't quite make out.

"No, I don't mind. But to tell you the truth, it makes me feel a little self-conscious."

"Why's that?"

"Because I have no credentials as a poet, and my poems seem pretty insignificant to me. Plus I never let anyone read my stuff, except for Saké, who just went right ahead."

Chokichi chuckled.

"What does that even *mean*, to 'have credentials as a poet,' huh? You write poetry... Shouldn't that be enough?"

"Well... er... yes. No. I don't know."

"You're gonna say that I don't know anything about literature, but I think you're being hard on yourself. Unlike Saké, I don't think you could make a living at it. We both agree on that. I'm just saying you should keep writing. I really liked what I read so far."

"Thank you. I'll keep at it, sure... but I need a project, something to keep me busy. I can't just listen to music all day and write poetry all night. But I wouldn't want to go to work just to kill time, you know? I need to be passionate about something. That's why I decided to follow Saké to California in the first place. Because she was inviting me on this crazy, outlandish adventure. Now, though—and I'm not blaming either of you—I feel like I'm wasting my time, just when I happen to have so much of it on my hands."

"You already have something in mind, eh?"

It was as if he'd read my mind.

"Yes."

"And it would mean you'd have to leave?"

I nodded.

I turned to him and kissed him. It was the first time *I* had kissed *him*. Right then, Saké burst into the room.

"You guys!" she cried, waving an envelope.

We straightened up and Saké sat down beside us on the bed.

"It's my folks. Again. But different this time. Read it."

She tossed the envelope our way. I opened it and read the message out loud.

Saké. Here's a little something for your living expenses, as well as for Chokichi and Hollywood. Sending hugs to all three of you.

There were ten one-thousand dollar bills, US. Nothing else.

Chokichi took the money and counted it a few times.

"Ten thousand bucks," he said. "Ten grand!"

Saké didn't look amused. Chokichi asked her what was wrong.

"My parents shouldn't know I live here. They shouldn't know your name, Chokichi. They shouldn't know that Hollywood is here either. And they never had this much cash. We always had enough to eat, but we never went on vacation and didn't own our home. Ever since they left, it's like... I keep discovering all the things they were hiding from me the whole time. Like they were actually loaded, waiting for the right moment to hit the road and blow all their cash. OK, sure, it bothers me a bit that they disappeared, but not enough to throw a fit or whatever. What annoys me is that they can always find me, no matter where I go; I can't leave without a trace, like they did. I don't get it..."

She collapsed on the bed and rested her head on my lap.

"With all the money they sent, plus Chokichi's pay, minus rent, food and travel, that leaves us about thirteen thousand dollars. I say we do something big. Something memorable. Something just for us."

Chokichi jumped to his feet.

"Thirteen thousand bucks. That's a ton of cash!" He was clearly excited about the whole thing. "We have to celebrate!"

He ran out of the room and came back a minute later holding a bottle of rum, two bags of chips and a huge chocolate bar.

"We don't have caviar or champagne, but at least we've got rum. I didn't bring the cucumbers," he said, winking at Saké.

"That's OK. I'm done with cucumbers. Pass me the chips!"

He tossed her the bag of prawn crackers, her favourite. He opened the bottle, took a swig and passed it around. I got up to put a new record on. I paused to think before choosing. Then I cleared my throat: "I picked a very special album for the occasion," I announced. "It might surprise you; it's not the type of music I tend to talk about. I found it at the music store over at the Plaza Center, the one on the corner of Hughes and Browns Ferry Road, and I bought it right away because it was the group's only album I didn't have. OK, so the others are in Montreal, but in any case, I love their stuff, and didn't own this particular one yet. It's their first, as it happens. I listen to these guys whenever I feel like spacing out and totally disconnecting from the real world that I just can't shake. So to celebrate our new-found fortune, I propose we listen to Wu-Tang Clan's *Enter the Wu-Tang (36 Chambers)*."

I brought the needle down on the first groove of *Bring da Ruckus*. I waited for the voiceover from *Shaolin & Wu Tang* (the movie) to end and then I closed my eyes. When Ghostface Killah began to sing, I started dancing. Saké screamed.

She and Chokichi started laughing. They got up to join me at the turntable with the bottle of rum. The three of us danced until five the next morning. Three bottles of rum later, Chokichi threw up and Saké fell asleep on the bedroom floor. When Chokichi crashed on the bathroom floor, I sat down at the kitchen table with my little notebook.

Hollywood

UNDERGROUND POEM #37

staring out the window at the yellow morn
stifling daylight
morning smog

I belong to the red-eyed people, a sleepless tribe

Xavier

AS WELL AS ZOOEY DESCHANEL MOVIES, I watched *Eternal Sunshine of the Spotless Mind* and *Dedication,* thinking about the dunes half covered in snow and the deserted beaches, the ghost towns, abandoned by Manhattanites who usually flock to them the moment their overpopulated island becomes stifling. It was enough to convince me that the trip to Montauk would be worth it. I rented a small cottage that wasn't quite as fancy as the beach house, without the piano or the envelope full of cash (theoretically, at least); a pretty little cottage with a wood-burning stove and French doors. I bought a few things, packed my bags and left on the morning of the third day, Wednesday.

The snow had stopped the previous day, as if to make way for me. It was cold, minus fifteen, but the road was cleared and it wasn't too difficult to get out of Pittsburgh. I left mid-morning, around nine thirty, to avoid traffic. I stopped twice for gas and food. On the way, I listened to NPR and the three *She & Him* albums. I crossed Pennsylvania heading east, then hit New Jersey. As I drove over the George Washington Bridge, I noticed that the Hudson River was still frozen. As was the Harlem River, under the Alexander Hamilton Bridge. I crossed the Bronx. Night had fallen. A few boats bobbed sleepily in the Long Island Sound. I took different highways to get to Route 27, which I followed all the way to Montauk, sometimes in the express lane, sometimes via the scenic route.

I got into town around 10 p.m. I drove through it slowly, going less than forty kilometres an hour. It felt weird to see the neon lights of the stores and the windows of houses still lit up. Cars drove down the streets, pedestrians walked along the sidewalks; the town had come back to life. I passed the pharmacy and I wanted to laugh, remembering my bruised shoulder. I realized that the pain hadn't followed me, that it had stayed in the dream. Then I pulled up in front of the cottage. I found the key under the mat, as the owner had said I would. I went in.

I lit a fire in the big wood stove and went to get my bags from the car. I dropped my things in what would be my bedroom for the next two weeks.

After I explored the house, I put on my coat and went out. The sky was clear, the wind had died down, a big moon was shining over the water and the little ripples expired almost soundlessly on the sand. All things considered, it wasn't too cold: about minus ten degrees Celsius.

I looked up to the sky; there was a clear view of Venus and Jupiter. I'd read something in the papers about it: these days, it seemed, we could thank our "lucky stars" that we were able to see five planets. I gazed at the sky long enough to see Jupiter move past Venus and climb higher in the celestial sphere; then the moon swung round to hover between the two planets. It all seemed to be happening at breakneck speed, but when I checked my phone I realized that I'd already been sitting on the little porch for nearly three hours. The movements of the planets and stars fascinated me. I set my phone on the ground and continued to watch the show. Every so often shooting stars would streak across the sky, and each time I'd make the same dumb wish: *I want to be happy, I want to be happy, I want to be happy.* I told myself that I was the only thing holding myself back, but I desperately asked the stars that fell into the sea: *Please, little celestial bodies, please. Make me happy.*

Then I noticed four bright spots surrounding Jupiter. One on the left, and three on the right. I picked up my phone and went online and discovered they were moons: Europa, Ganymede, Io and Callisto. I immediately thought back to the TV documentary that I'd watched a few times. I ran inside the cottage; the lights were all out and the fire in the wood stove had turned to embers. I rekindled it with logs and dry wood, then rummaged through the living room, kitchen and nook, where I finally found what I was looking for: an old shortwave radio. I opened all the kitchen drawers and grabbed a roll of aluminum foil and some alkaline batteries. I went back outside.

I changed the batteries and put together a makeshift antenna with the foil, taking care to split it in two after a bit and connect it to the coaxial cable. I turned on the radio and twisted the dial to change the frequency. I went too far: after 26 MHz I started to pick up truck drivers and the local police. I went back down to about 20 MHz. Then I landed on the right frequency: live from Jupiter, a sound like crashing waves mixed with forlorn whale songs. I lay down on my back, my eyes trained on Io, and I listened to the planet sing for a long time while I cried like a baby.

A thud from the radio woke me with a start. I waited a few seconds, motionless, hoping to hear it again so I could try and figure out what it was, but nothing. That's when I realized: I'd been sleeping. I got out my phone to check the time. It was dead, so I had no idea how long I'd been out. I switched the radio to FM and searched in vain for a 24-hour news station that could give me the time. The only stations I picked up were playing classical music. I turned off the radio and got up.

I spun around to head back to the cottage, but it was no longer there. The beach house stood in front of me, just as I remembered it. The same one I had drawn in my notebook.

Hollywood

AROUND NINE O'CLOCK, I heard Chokichi get up and go lie down in the bedroom. At eleven, Saké walked into the kitchen. She virtually downed a tall glass of water and stretched for a good ten minutes before opening her mouth.

"Morning."

"Morning."

She guffawed.

"Do you want something to eat?"

"Sure! Why not?"

"Don't you feel sick?"

"Nah, I'm all right. I wasn't *that* drunk... What knocked me out was all the dancing—and then the bedroom floor."

I made breakfast while she read what I'd written overnight. I made toast, fried eggs and bacon, and cooked breakfast potatoes from the freezer. Chokichi had been allowed to fill our fridge and shelves with 'real food' after finding out Saké's diet was nothing but a lie. The smell woke him. He dragged himself into the kitchen and groaned as he sank into a chair.

"I know I was sick yesterday, but I'm hungry now and my head is killing me, so you're gonna give me something to eat. And Saké, you're gonna let me have some of your headache pills. Right?"

Ever since Saké had confiscated his gear, she'd been in charge of our medicine box, which she kept hidden somewhere among her things. She got up without saying a word and came back with two ibuprofen tablets for Chokichi.

"Thanks," he said, washing them down with a big gulp from my glass of water.

I made breakfast for Chokichi too, and we all sat down to eat. It had been a rough night. We'd danced the whole time, and all we needed now was to recharge our batteries, which is exactly what we did as we stuffed our faces.

"This is a nice change from cucumbers and herbs," said Chokichi, his irony aimed at Saké.

"Ha, ha," she answered, munching on a piece of toast. "Shut up and eat."

Watching them tease each other like that made me smile: I'd never have guessed the three of us would be living together so soon, in a place as strange as Madison, Alabama; or that Saké would be singing the national anthem before softball games; or that Chokichi would be turning to the fast-food industry to buy me records; or that I would be writing lame poems every single night, watching the stars through the kitchen window. Which reminded me I had an announcement to make.

"I have to tell you something..."

Saké cut me off without looking up from her plate.

"You want to leave. I know."

Chokichi put his fork down and looked me in the eye.

"I do. But I want you guys to come with me. I know how we should spend our thirteen thousand dollars. And even if we didn't have this much cash, I'd still ask you guys to come along. This isn't about the money."

Chokichi smiled. He seemed relieved by what I'd just said. I don't know if he really doubted my intentions, but it had been clear to me for a while now that I could never leave without them.

"Where do you want to go?" Saké asked.

"Montauk."

"Montauk? Where the hell is that?" asked Chokichi.

"In the Hamptons, at the tip of Long Island. About two hundred kilometres from New York."

They didn't need much convincing after I gave them a rough idea of the kind of place it was. Saké was won over when I told her Montauk was full of rich, upper-class people, artists and intellectuals who fled the city for the summer, and Chokichi was tempted by the sea, the beaches and the wind. But I still had to lay out my project, my plan, the reason I wanted to leave Madison, Alabama, and move to Montauk. It meant I'd have to tell them about Xavier, the hotel rooms and the beach house, and I didn't want to. I wanted to keep all that to myself. That way, I'd be the only one disappointed if my plan didn't work out—if I could never fall asleep again, or meet Xavier, or contact him again. I'd spent a long time thinking it through, until I came up with another reason for us to move to Montauk. That's the one I decided to use.

"I've spent of lot of sleepless nights surfing the net. I joined a couple of birding forums. More and more rare birds have been spotted near Montauk over the past few months. Yellow-billed loons, for instance. They're water-birds that typically breed in the Arctic tundra and winter on the coasts of Norway, the Pacific Ocean, Japan and off the Kamchatka Peninsula. They usually nest in northern Canada and Russia after the ice melts, but close to a dozen of them have been spotted in Montauk over the last five months, which is making some people think they might not be lost or blown off course but actually settling in the Hamptons. I've also seen pictures of Western tanagers, which are normally found in coniferous forests across western North America. And another polar bird, the king eider, has been spotted three or four times off Montauk Point. Climate change is affecting North American birds: these species aren't usually that far east or south. And because it's been so warm for so long, other species have been spotted in Montauk, as if they all decided to meet up there: a blue-throated macaw; an endangered Bolivian bird; and two purple-collared woodstars, which usually live in Peru and Ecuador. And get this: last week at Deep Hollow Ranch, a birder from New York spotted and photographed a couple of three-banded plovers from Madagascar. A whole team of volunteers is now combing the beach for nests, because these particular plovers are known to nest right on the shingles. I got in touch with the secretary of the New York State Ornithological Association, and he's expecting us next week. We'll be helping them with their research, taking notes, gathering evidence, guano, pieces of straw, that kind of thing. We'll take pictures of birds, record data in notebooks and save it all on the computer, making the research results and discoveries available to all. We won't get paid, but the man I talked to gave me a few useful addresses. I found a small house to rent on the beach, not too far from town, within easy walking distance. Come on, pack up! We're off to Montauk to do some birdwatching!"

"Here we go..." Chokichi groaned.

::

We moved to Montauk exactly a week after I first brought up the idea. First, Chokichi got us a used car, an old clunker that was falling to pieces but still running and could probably make it all the way to Montauk. Chokichi was quite clear when he told the owner of the scrapyard we had a thousand miles to drive, but the guy insisted that the car would make it. "It may not go a lot further than that, but it'll do the job. It's a good car," he said. Chokichi gave him three hundred-dollar bills in exchange for the keys, which, as it turns out, could only start the engine: the car doors wouldn't lock. Saké went to tell the landlord we were leaving. We crammed our things into a few suitcases, the most unwieldy being the turntable. We packed up the car, bought food and gas for the trip and we were on our way. The sun was still blazing hot—one hundred degrees Fahrenheit—and the old brown clunker didn't have AC. We drove for a couple of hours with the windows down and the radio up full blast, the static so loud we could sometimes barely hear whatever song was playing. Saké was in charge of the radio and only picked country music stations.

"We're off on our American road trip, full speed or nothing!" she yelled, her hair blowing in the wind and enormous sunglasses covering her face.

In Chattanooga, we took Interstate 75 and drove up to the outskirts of Knoxville, Tennessee, where the engine died on us. Saké got out of the car and started waving her arms about, hoping someone would pull over and help us out. A mechanic, who was on his way home after his shift, stopped by the side of the road and took a look at the motor.

"That car ain't worth shit, bro," he said to Chokichi. "No way you can make it with that pile o' junk. The engine's dead, man."

He called a colleague of his, who came to pick us up in his tow truck. He drove us to the scrapyard, where we waved a fistful of bills in the owner's face. He sold us another, less beat-up ride. We'd wasted two hours of our time and close to five hundred dollars on this little adventure. Chokichi was sulking, but Saké, in her infinite wisdom, convinced him that it wasn't the end of the world, that the birds could wait, that her folks would no doubt find a way to track us down and pay us back and more within a week or two. We still had about twelve thousand dollars left anyway; it wasn't as if we were about to run out of money anytime soon.

We got back on the road, and Chokichi drove straight to Roanoke, Virginia, where we stopped to have a bite to eat, go to the bathroom and look on a map to see how far was left to Montauk. We decided to call it a day and spend the night in a motel. We still had a ten-hour drive ahead of us.

And off we went the next day, stopping only once for food and gas. We reached Montauk in the late evening. About eighty-five degrees (thirty degrees Celsius) under a starry sky. The damp air clung to our skin, but the sea breeze made it bearable. All three of us went to explore the house we'd rented for the next six months: two bedrooms with splendid bay windows, a wide porch, an open-plan kitchen and living room, a fireplace and a piano. I'd deliberately rented a place that reminded me of the beach house as much as possible. In fact, our house *was* on the beach, separated from the ocean by dunes covered with tall yellow grass.

Chokichi and I picked the bedroom with a view of the dunes, and Saké settled into the one overlooking the long private lane leading to Surfside Avenue. Chokichi cooked us a light meal that we ate sitting on the wooden floor of the porch. The air smelled of salt and seawater, and the wind blew through our hair, caressing our faces, and everything was so perfect that I felt like screaming.

As the sun was setting behind our house, the stars blinked on one after the other. The moon came into sight: a big white orb emerging from the depths of the ocean.

We discussed our game plan for a while: we had the whole weekend to get to know the area before starting to work for the Ornithological Association. Saké wanted us to visit the town and search the house, hunting for old treasures. Chokichi and I didn't have any special requests, so we settled on going to town on Saturday and exploring the house and our surroundings the next day. Saké was satisfied with our plan. She walked back inside and went to bed. Chokichi was tired too.

"I'll catch up with you in a bit," I said. "I just want to look at the stars a while longer."

He kissed me before following Saké inside. I stepped off the porch and went to lie down on the dunes, gazing at the sky. I did a little mapping exercise and located Orion's Belt, the Big Dipper, Venus and Jupiter.

I lay there, completely still, for a few minutes or hours. I was unaware of the passage of time. I watched Jupiter going past Venus, and the rising moon becoming smaller and smaller. I also counted shooting stars, but stopped once I got over fifty. I'd never heard of such an impressive meteor shower. Then I thought it might be normal that I should see so many here, where there was less light pollution than in the city. At a certain point, I thought I heard something fall into the water nearby, as if another meteor had hit the Earth. But since the stone had probably ended up in the ocean, there was no way I could ever find it.

I started paying a little more attention to the light reflecting off Jupiter. I noticed, after closely observing that part of the sky, that its four moons were visible: Callisto, Io, Ganymede and Europa. I was immediately reminded of the documentary I'd seen several times on TV, and had a sudden urge to try and listen for Jupiter on the radio, like they said you could on the show. I went into the house and rummaged through the closets, but couldn't find a radio. I went back out, resolving to buy one in town as soon as possible so I could do the experiment.

I was suddenly woken by a rumbling noise, followed by a muffled explosion; until then, I wasn't even aware that I'd fallen asleep. I got to my feet and realized that a hole had appeared on the beach, in the sand, less than ten metres away. There was smoke coming from the small crater. I knew what it was right away. I got closer to confirm my hunch: once again, a star had fallen right next to me. I wondered if Chokichi and Saké had been woken by the blast. I turned around.

I was standing before the beach house—the *real* beach house—and Xavier was sitting on the porch, poring over a piece of paper he was holding.

Epilogue

Montauk

Boys, I knew you would eventually end up meeting here. There's something I would like to tell you.

Hollywood, do you remember that party at your friend Chokichi's, at the end of August? It was much too hot, and you'd taken something, maybe ecstasy, I'm not sure. I was there because I'd been invited by a friend. A cousin of Chokichi's. Anyway... I was your one-night stand, the girl you shed so many tears over. You had a son, Zarik, but he's no longer with us. Xavier can explain.

Xavier, i dashur, don't worry. Yesterday was the last day of cold. In Montauk, the weather will never change, you'll see. You'll be able to look at the stars as much as you like. And at the sea, for me.

The air will always be a bit chilly. But the grass will grow tall. And there will be birds.

Love,
Gia

Xavier

It's like waking up after a dream and finding it hard to shake the feeling. The dream was so realistic that it's difficult to distinguish one from the other, the true from the false. And on what basis can we judge if something is true or not, anyway? If I perceive it, it must exist. This knowledge is reassuring; it's like a cogito that keeps me from going crazy, from falling too far out of step with the world. But sometimes you get lost.

Ultimately, I'm just a needle in a haystack.

We must agree to go back to where we started.

Hollywood

UNDERGROUND POEM
UNNUMBERED

when it is time to start over
with no start or end in sight
I lie down on the roof of the world

you may commit your own murder

Pierre-Luc Landry

THIS NOVEL WAS BORN IN THE CAFÉ DE PARIS restrooms of the Montreal Ritz-Carlton. Next to a room full of politicians, actresses and great writers, I was locked up in a stall, sipping a glass of white wine—my third... or was it my fourth?—scribbling on hotel paper with the pencil I'd borrowed. That was nearly seven years ago. I work slowly, but always with a sense of urgency, and at the very last minute.

I wrote this book so that I could go on exploring through fiction the topics I am obsessed with: existence, strangeness, how each of us experiences reality and the world around us. I wanted to think about truth for a while, the kind of truth we cling to in specific circumstances. Because, for me, the "purpose" of fiction is not to create a different world; I don't write to make things up, but to describe some reality, a thing that already exists.

Listening for Jupiter is my second attempt at doing just that. I think it's possible, through fiction, to dig deeper into the so-called "literary." In order to do so, you have to keep pushing back its limits and those of the genre itself: the novel as a well-written, well-told, well-structured piece. I'm not sure whether I've succeeded or not. But it may not even be relevant to wonder, since no book alone could help achieve such a goal—unless its author is a genius, which I'm not and don't claim to be. Still. It would be so much simpler...

QC Fiction brings you the very best of a new generation of Quebec storytellers, sharing surprising, interesting novels in flawless English translation.

Available from QC Fiction:

1. *LIFE IN THE COURT OF MATANE* by Eric Dupont
(translated by Peter McCambridge)

2. *THE UNKNOWN HUNTSMAN* by Jean-Michel Fortier
(translated by Katherine Hastings)

3. *BROTHERS* by David Clerson
(translated by Katia Grubisic)

4. *LISTENING FOR JUPITER* by Pierre-Luc Landry
(translated by Arielle Aaronson and Madeleine Stratford)

Coming soon from QC Fiction:

5. *I NEVER TALK ABOUT IT* by Véronique Côté and Steve Gagnon
(translated by 37 different translators)

6. *BEHIND THE EYES WE MEET* by Mélissa Verreault
(translated by Arielle Aaronson)

7. *A MADELEINE OF ONE'S OWN* by Eric Dupont
(translated by Peter McCambridge)

8. *AN EXPLOSIVE MIND: MICHAEL BAY
AND THE PYROTECHNICS OF THE IMAGINATION*
by Mathieu Poulin
(translated by Aleshia Jensen)

Visit **qcfiction.com** for details and to subscribe
to a full season of QC Fiction titles.

Printed in April 2017
by Gauvin Press,
Gatineau, Québec